D1344297

WHAT WOULD *YOU* BID?

also by Terence Reese (and others)

THE COMPLETE BOOK OF BRIDGE
(with Albert Dormer)

THE BRIDGE PLAYER'S ALPHABETICAL HANDBOOK
(with Albert Dormer)

THE BLUE CLUB
(adapted from the French)

OMAR SHARIF'S LIFE IN BRIDGE
(adapted from the French)

BRIDGE — THE MODERN GAME
(with David Bird)

HOW THE EXPERTS DO IT
(with David Bird)

LEARN BRIDGE WITH REESE

What Would *You* Bid?

TERENCE REESE

faber and faber

LONDON · BOSTON

First published in 1986 by
Faber and Faber Limited
3 Queen Square London WC1N 3AU

Photoset by Wilmaset Birkenhead Wirral
Printed in Great Britain by
Richard Clay Ltd Bungay Suffolk
All rights reserved

© Terence Reese 1986

British Library Cataloguing in Publication Data

Reese, Terence
What would you bid?
1. Contract bridge—Bidding
I. Title
795.41'52   GV1282.4

ISBN 0–571–14596–5

Contents

Foreword

Like many readers of the bridge magazines, I dare say, I always turn first to the bidding competition, which is usually both entertaining and instructive. It is surprising that no one so far has thought of basing a book on this feature.

Once a fair standard has been reached, nothing makes a bigger difference to a player's score than good judgement in tricky situations where a bidding system will not supply the answer. I have concentrated on problems of this kind.

Always consider your own answer – write it down – before reading any further. You cannot 'learn' judgement, but you can certainly develop it by studying the reasons that good players put forward for making a particular bid in a particular situation. The fact that they often disagree with one another is beside the point.

Many of the magazines have changed their titles and format over the years. Of those from which I have quoted (with permission) in this book, the following are alive and well:

Bridge International, £16.95 annually (12 issues), from 30 Fleet St, London EC4.

International Popular Bridge Monthly (IPBM), £15, from 32 The Ropewalk, Nottingham NG1.

Bridge World, $27 (rate for overseas), from 39 West 94th St, New York, NY 10025.

Australian Bridge, $A33 airmail, from PO Box 246, Port Melbourne 3207.

David Bird, author of the fine Monastery stories, read the first draft of this book and made many valuable observations. He also drew my attention to a few passages that he considered somewhat eccentric. That was the intention, I told him.

PART I
TACTICS AND STRATAGEMS

Australian Bridge
Director: Keith McNeil

Pairs, E–W vul. You, South, hold:

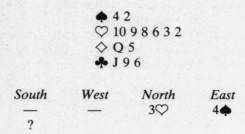

♠ 4 2
♡ 10 9 8 6 3 2
♢ Q 5
♣ J 9 6

South	West	North	East
—	—	3♡	4♠
?			

Readers who are accustomed to bidding competitions will recognize this type of problem. Once in a Gold Cup match, John Pugh, knowing that his side was outgunned, *doubled* the intervention. It was a clever move, because the opposition might well miss an easy slam, gaining less from the doubled overtricks. If they redouble, South will of course take flight.

Whether or not they were familiar with the original occasion, a few panelists – well, three out of thirty-two – were on this trail.

BELLADONNA: Double. I save in front of the slam. If the opponents redouble I bid five hearts and hope that the fish will bite the hook.

KOKISH: Double. It's a dream to believe that the opponents won't do the right thing here if we fool around or bash. They have just too much fire-power. If I double them, however, they may forget to redouble and score only 1390. If they redouble I can guess *how* to run.

REESE: Double. I have never actually made a striped-tail-ape double and have almost forgotten what it means; but this must be the moment.

(The phrase 'striped-tail-ape' signifies the hasty disappearance should an opponent redouble.)

The Director was happy with these answers, but also gave credit to some alternatives.

LAVINGS: 7♡. They make at least six spades, so make them guess whether to bid seven spades or not.

COURTNEY: 7♡. Give them the hardest guess. I'm hoping they bid seven spades and these lower honours in the minors could result in a trick (or two). At pairs they may well bid seven spades on the spurious reasoning that they are fixed anyway.

Another possibility is to pass over four spades. The case for this was well put by several panelists.

MARSTON: Pass. Whatever they bid they will probably make, so it's important that you *don't* bid. Your action will help them by announcing the heart fit and it will give them impetus. Players generally overbid in competitive situations.

ALDER: Pass. One should not lurch skywards in hearts because one will tell the opponents that their hands are fitting well. It is possible that West is about to pass. Second choice, seven hearts. There is no point in half measures.

CUMMINGS: Pass. Any 'funny' action could work, depending on the company. A direct leap to six hearts should get zero as you *force* them to a cold small slam or grand slam.

McNeil agreed with this. [NOTE: COMMENTS IN ITALIC ARE ALWAYS THOSE OF THE DIRECTOR.]

Director: Yep – a direct leap to six or seven hearts will almost certainly see them bidding on and I lack any faith in the trick-taking potential of the minors.

There were supporters for both five hearts and six hearts:

GILL: 5♡. Simply hoping for a rhythmic five spades, passed out. Will later save in seven hearts if necessary.

Seems to me that this approach has a lot of merit.

Not to me; the opponents have so much strength between them that if they touch five spades they will surely go to six – at least.

KANTAR: 6♡. At least I have cut out Blackwood and the Grand Slam Force.

True, but would not five hearts achieve the same result?

Actually, no; there is still room for 5NT by West – or five spades by West and 5NT by East.

TRAVIS (Barbara): 4NT. The tactical bid, then seven hearts over six spades, praying partner has a trick.

4NT might prove a success in the qualifying round of the Ladies Pairs; not elsewhere.

This was the marking:

CALL	AWARD	PANEL
Pass	100	9
Double	90	3
7♡	80	7
5♡	70	2
6♡	60	6
Others	50	5

While I voted for Double – if only to show that I hadn't forgotten this tactical manoeuvre – I think that the arguments for Pass are stronger. The point is that West, with fair values, may then pass also; once he enters the bidding, the partnership will surely go to slam. Also, if you pass and West bids freely, you are still there; you may be able to gauge whether they are likely to advance to seven spades over seven hearts.

2

IPBM

Director: Joe Amsbury

Rubber bridge, both vul. You, South, hold:

♠ A
♡ A
♢ K Q 10
♣ A K Q 8 7 6 4 2

South	West	North	East
—	—	—	No
?			

You may say, 'I never get a hand like this at rubber Bridge.'
Perhaps not, but one day you might and the point of the
problem is to judge the best way to deal with a freakish hand of
this nature. There were two main groups, starting with:

KELSEY: 2♣. If the diamond ace is missing I am prepared to
chance six clubs so long as my hand is concealed. The
trouble with an opening 4NT is that partner will get in the
club bid first.

ROWLANDS: 2♣. Could open 4NT, but pard might respond five
clubs and become declarer. If pard has nothing in
diamonds the hand will be somewhat easier to defend when
the big hand is exposed.

SOLOWAY: 2♣. My first instinct was to bid 4NT, Blackwood,
and then bid six clubs over five clubs, but my hand would
be exposed. This way (opening 2♣), I get to play six clubs.
Will bid Blackwood at my earliest opportunity.

WOLFF: 2♣. We could bid six clubs, but what about seven? We
can't shut opponents out.

Director: Certainly not via 2♣.
I suspect that Bobby Wolff's reply may have been abbreviated.

The majority favoured a direct 4NT. Thus:

STABELL: 4NT. Asking for specific aces.

SHEEHAN: 4NT. Educated partners cue-bid the ace of diamonds. Uneducated ones show one ace.

So you're all right either way, he means. The old Acol idea was that over an opening 4NT the responder should name the ace he held (five clubs with no ace, six clubs with the ace of clubs).

ARMSTRONG: 4NT. Who knows what the best tactical approach is? I follow a simple approach.

Well, you said it.

FORRESTER: 4NT. Surely even rubber-bridge players know what this means. At least I have ten tricks in my own hand just in case. I have now bid 4NT four times in bidding competitions and never at the table – says much for the type of problem one gets.

Simple enough, Tony. At the table you have a lot of armoury; here you have minimum system, maximum common sense.

He means that panelists cannot base their answers on under-standings they may have with a particular partner. Needless to say, this Director's notion of maximum common sense is not universally agreed.

KOKISH: 4NT. It lives and breathes: an opening Blackwood space-stealer, and hopefully not a flag-waver . . .

He interprets the opening 4NT in a Blackwood, not the old Acol, sense. (As for the use of 'hopefully' for 'one hopes', one hopes that this usage will eventually pass away.)

PRICE: 4NT. Intending to play in six or seven clubs. With a known partner I might open two clubs, intending to discover if there is a diamond suit opposite.

6

Curious observation.

The Director originally favoured 4NT, it seems, but observed politely: *Looks so obvious, but I was seduced away from 4NT.*

The seduction arose from:

REESE: 6♣. Would rather miss seven than give them a chance to sacrifice. Also, concealing your hand may help in the play.

There you see the commercial attitude of two players who in their time have played rubber bridge for the rent.

This was the marking:

CALL	AWARD	PANEL
4NT	10	11
2♣	6	8
6♣	6	2

The other vote for six clubs was from 'Palooka', a known contributor who likes to play the part of the non-expert. His sage comment on this occasion was not quoted.

3

Bridge Magazine
Director: Eric Milnes

IMPs, both vul. You, South, hold:

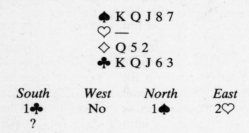

♠ K Q J 8 7
♡ —
♦ Q 5 2
♣ K Q J 6 3

South	West	North	East
1♣	No	1♠	2♡
?			

You can show your heart void in one way or another, or jump in spades, or make a tactical bid of some kind. All these moves were suggested in the panel's answers.

Eric Milnes, who now, alas, is no longer with us, was a bluff Yorkshireman, a good writer and a capable, if not expert, player. His bidding feature was shorter than most, and his comments were usually brief. All he said about this problem was:

Director: Whereas three hearts at this stage could mean one or two things, four hearts is totally unambiguous.

Unambiguous it may be, but does it give an accurate picture of the values, or lack of them? No aces and possibly three losers in diamonds. Jack Marx supported the bid in venerable prose.

MARX: 4♡. Such a jump cue-bid will always affirm a first-round control – more usually than not, a void. There are players who may consider such a bid without an outside ace to be too forward-going, but there is no other way to convey the precise message that West wishes to impart.

On the same side:

BENJAMIN: 4♥. Setting the trump suit and guaranteeing first-round control.

MOELLER: 4♥. I am skating on thin ice, not being accustomed to cue-bids. This sounds like a void-showing cue-bid, but does partner expect more first-round controls?

With a happy vision:

VON DEWITZ: 3♥. And after four diamonds, six spades.

Others who voted for three hearts, Fox, Auhagen, Martin Cohn, Victor Mollo, did not declare their future hopes or intentions. Jean Besse, Bob Rowlands and Alan Hiron proposed four spades, perhaps because they thought it wise to keep the heart void up their sleeves, or perhaps because they did not want to give an exaggerated impression of their strength.

Which, in my opinion, is what four hearts does. I can well imagine this leading to an insecure contract at the five level. I held the hand myself, playing with Irving Rose, and made the bid that I think he would have chosen, to wit:

Reese adopts a crafty line.

REESE: 2♠. It pays to be cunning with this type. For one thing, if you leap to game you will encourage them to lead diamonds, not hearts.

This was the marking:

CALL	AWARD	PANEL
4♥	10	8
3♥	8	5
4♠	7	3
3♠	2	1
2♠	2	1

This Director's marking was generally in proportion to the panel's votes.

Three spades was Le Dentu's suggestion. This was a good answer because now, if you follow with four spades in a competitive auction, you may be allowed to play there.

When you have powerful distribution but no aces, and can be sure that the opponents will compete further, it is good tactics to underbid.

4

British Bridge World
Director: Albert Dormer

IMPs, E–W vul. You, South, hold:

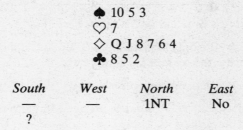

♠ 10 5 3
♡ 7
♢ Q J 8 7 6 4
♣ 8 5 2

South	West	North	East
—	—	1NT	No
?			

The 1NT opening is in the 12–14 range. Nowadays, many
players use transfer sequences when responding to 1NT, but
these were not in common use when the problem was posed.
Assume, therefore, that you are playing with an unfamiliar
partner and have not come to any arrangement about responses
to 1NT.

The hand 'belongs' to the opposition, obviously, and you
have to decide on the best defensive, or obstructive, tactics.

*Director: It is generally reckoned that a player is entitled to
considerable licence in this kind of position. It is odds on
opponents having a vulnerable game and South has to consider
the best means of depriving them of their heritage. (Like a
wicked uncle.)*

SHARPLES: 3NT. The bigger the swindle, the smaller the
chance of detection. West will think twice before doubling,
not wishing to place the missing cards. If the worst
happens, four diamonds should not be disastrous.

It will be doubled and will probably cost 300 or more.

RODRIGUE: 3NT against good players who will not double just
   because 'I had 15 points, partner, I had to try it'; two
   spades against weaker players who are more likely to
   double 3NT on their 15 points. I consider two spades
   preferable to two hearts, as the likelihood is that they will
   run into a bad break if they play in this suit [hearts],
   whereas I know that the spades will break as favourably as
   possible for them.

*Topley (2NT) and North (Pass) make 3NT a close second
choice. Phillips's selection might be the best of all.*

PHILLIPS: 2♠, the only reasonably safe bid that stands a chance
   of silencing the opponents completely.

I rate that better than the next offering.

SWINNERTON-DYER: 2♡. Some years ago Meredith bid 3NT on
   a hand very like this and went down six, undoubled,
   chuckling happily at every 50. [Not correct: he would have
   looked increasingly grave.] Since then the 3NT call has
   been part of every expert's equipment. The opportunity
   does not come up very often, of course; indeed, it has not
   come up again yet, and when it does I expect the result will
   cause this coup to be forgotten hurriedly.
      All the same, we must do something: they must have a
   vulnerable game on. The best hope is to persuade West,
   who probably holds hearts, that the hand is a misfit and
   that he should sit back and watch me sweat. Very few pairs
   have agreed that a double, in West's position, would be for
   penalties.

Swinnerton-Dyer often supplied original, and sometimes brilliant, answers, but this one strikes me as an outstanding
example of academic folly. (He was soon to become Master of
Trinity College, Cambridge.) To begin with, why do they all
assume that opponents are cold for a game, and also that they
are likely to bid it? They have presumably about 24 points

between them, and this is an area where much sparring takes place after the opening 1NT. Also, if they play in four hearts they may run into a 4–1 trump break; and if they play in four spades there is the possibility of a heart ruff.

And if you *are* nervous, how can two hearts be remotely sensible? The main danger is that opponents will enter and that partner will compete to three hearts. By this time your side will be in the 300–500 zone, saving nothing.

This was the marking:

CALL	AWARD	PANEL
3NT	10	5
2♠	6	1
Pass	5	1
2♢	5	1
2♡	5	1
2NT	5	1
4♢	4	1

My own vote was for a passive two diamonds, because I did not think there was much danger that the opponents would bid and make a game. I think now that either Phillips's two spades or Pass would be better. The point is that if you respond two diamonds either West will double or the bidding will revert to East, and he will have enough to compete, either with a double or with two hearts. On the other hand, if you pass 1NT the last player will always be afraid that you are trapping, perhaps with a flat 10 or 11 points.

It is also fashionable these days to respond with a Stayman two clubs when you know that you are outgunned. You can hardly do that here, because the opener's rebid is likely to be two hearts. In some systems three diamonds, or 2NT as a (temporary) transfer to three clubs, would be a weak response. Whether such a move is better than a menacing pass is doubtful.

As for the popular 3NT, one danger is that East, having passed with good defensive prospects, may now double, and you will end with a heavy loss in four diamonds doubled.

5

Bridge World
Director: Howard Schenken

Rubber bridge, E–W vul. You, South, hold:

♠ 6 2
♥ K Q 9 7 3
♦ Q 5
♣ K Q 9 8

South	West	North	East
—	1◇	2♡	3◇
?			

Partner's jump overcall is weak in the American style and is unlikely to contain four spades, because in general it is considered undesirable to make a shut-out bid when holding length in both majors. Thus one of your tactical problems is to prevent the opponents from getting together in spades. You are playing rubber bridge, so you cannot draw any special inference from the fact that East has not made a negative double (as he might when holding four spades).

Director: The majority opinion was that South should do something about the spade situation.

WOLFF: 4♣. Some guile is called for. After a simple four hearts it will probably go four spades – pass – pass. Maybe something good will happen if I bid four clubs.

Something carefully left unspecified, however.

SUGAR: 5♡. An advance sacrifice against spades. Let them

guess at my level. At rubber bridge I can afford the extravagance.

Is that right? As Schenken points out, to save for 500 against a vulnerable game is good business at duplicate, but not at rubber bridge. The tactical objective here should be to obtain the contract, if you can, at four hearts. The majority view was expressed by:

TSCHEKALOFF: 4♡. Before the opponents can discover their spade fit.

I am in the four-heart camp. The opponents may be forced to double at this level and a four-spade bid by West may be interpreted as a cue-bid. (It ought not to be in a competitive situation like this, but such things do happen.) *Still others felt that the most confusing action would be the best.*

DONNELLY: 4NT, to block out an anticipated spade call by West. A three-spade psychic would not be effective against experienced opponents.

I dare say not, but would 4NT daunt them?

Finally, one group of sneaks plays it cosy by passing.

ROTH: Pass. I believe the opponents have a game, whether in spades or diamonds. My experience shows that opener may pass three diamonds.

RUBENS: Pass. Over a heart raise East–West will surely bid spades. If I pass, spade bids may sound like notrump tries.

KAPLAN: Pass. I have enough points to give hope that the opponents will underbid if I keep quiet and don't tell them about their perfect fit. Somehow, it's harder for opener to bid spades over partner's diamonds than over my hearts.

This problem was taken from a rubber bridge game in New York. On that occasion the full deal was:

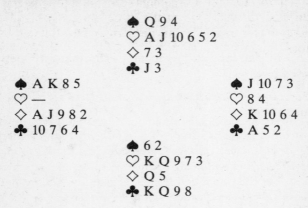

♠ Q 9 4
♡ A J 10 6 5 2
♢ 7 3
♣ J 3

♠ A K 8 5   ♠ J 10 7 3
♡ —   ♡ 8 4
♢ A J 9 8 2   ♢ K 10 6 4
♣ 10 7 6 4   ♣ A 5 2

♠ 6 2
♡ K Q 9 7 3
♢ Q 5
♣ K Q 9 8

As can be seen, East–West can make five spades, but cannot make five diamonds. North–South can take eight tricks in hearts.

It seems to me that the deal leaves the basic issues unresolved. Would West bid if South passed three diamonds? Would West bid four spades if South bid four hearts? What would happen if South bid four clubs instead?

Five diamonds might, in fact, be made: duck a club, cash the ace, eliminate hearts, draw trumps, and throw North in on the third round of spades.

This was the marking:

CALL	AWARD	PANEL
4♡	100	12
4♣	90	8
5♡	80	5
5♣	80	2
4NT	80	1
Pass	50	5

The bids that take North–South beyond the level of four hearts all look wrong to me; as Howard Schenken remarked, there is nothing clever in conceding 500 at rubber bridge. Note that none of the panel made the obvious, but ill-judged, bid of three hearts. There are sound arguments for both four hearts and four clubs; and look again at the three quotes in favour of a pass; each makes a valid point, perhaps underestimated by the Director.

Bridge International
Director: Keith McNeil

Pairs, none vul. You, South, hold:

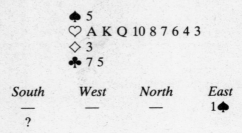

♠ 5
♡ A K Q 10 8 7 6 4 3
◇ 3
♣ 7 5

South	West	North	East
—	—	—	1♠
?			

You might think there wouldn't be much variation here – but you would be wrong. The experts found six different bids! The guest conductor (as I believe they say in the musical trade) began with the following remark:

Director: Problems like this tend to disclose the hidden personality of the panelist. Answers range from the frighteningly devious to the simple and obvious, and often provide great opportunities for lawyers specializing in slander.

ALDER: 5♡. What else? Even Jane Priday will do this.
PRIDAY (Jane): 4♡. Some panelists may consider this unimaginative, but they would be science-fiction addicts, which I'm not.

Also in the 'simple and obvious' camp:

REESE: 4♡. There is nothing clever in the Irving Rose ploy of passing and then attempting to 'surprise' at the five level. Sometimes they cannot bid over four hearts.

SHEEHAN: 4♥. Rose passes (a) to show how clever he is, and (b) to give East–West a chance to gauge their strength.

How to build partnership confidence!

With nine sure tricks it is clear that we are prepared to try and buy this hand at the five level. Sound pre-emptive tactics dictate that the players should make only the one bid at the highest level. Agreeing is:

SCHROEDER: 5♥. Since I always pre-empt only one time, I do it at the level where I want to defend.

Another school of thought tries to buy the contract at the four level, then is 'pushed' one more time, hoping thus to deceive the opposition.

LAVINGS: 4♥. But don't wince if I later bid five.
SOLOWAY: 4♥. Try to buy it at the four level, then can bid one more later.

Yet another theory exists, which advises allowing opponents to announce the level at which they want to play, and then sacrificing if necessary. The flaw in this, of course, is that our silence gives them all the room they need to exchange information. It allows them to gauge where their contract lies, making the decision to double or bid on much more likely to be correct.

SHARPLES: Pass. Too late to pre-empt against spades, so we may as well sit back and listen in to developments.

Then there is the sneak up on 'em approach, designed to induce a double later at some acceptable level by naïve opponents.

MOLLO: 2♥. I do not want to commit myself prematurely before there is an indication who has what.

And these two comments tickled the Director:

ROWLANDS: 2♥. Must preserve my reputation for sound over-calls.
WOLFF: 2♥. I hope I don't get doubled.

The Scientists must not be overlooked:

CROWHURST: 2♠. I like to play that an immediate overcall in the opponent's suit shows either a strong two-suited hand or a game-going one-suiter.

Finishing with the simple majority:

KELSEY: 4♡. A simple bid for simple players.
HAUSLER: 4♡. I'm too dumb for anything else.

This was the marking:

CALL	AWARD	PANEL
4♡	10	10
5♡	9	4
2♠	4	1
Pass	3	2
2♡	3	3
3♡	3	1

One objection to the sprightly five hearts, surely, is that partner may go down with something of this kind:

♠ Q J 9 x   ♡ x   ◇ K 10 x x   ♣ K Q x x

You could have made four hearts, they can't make anything, and you are one down doubled in five hearts. That is what would happen to me, anyway.

British Bridge World
Director: Alan Hiron

IMPs, N–S vul. You, South, hold:

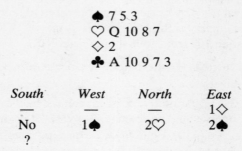

♠ 7 5 3
♡ Q 10 8 7
♢ 2
♣ A 10 9 7 3

South	West	North	East
—	—	—	1◇
No	1♠	2♡	2♠
?			

South would like to buy the contract in four hearts. What is the best way to achieve that objective? The Director began:

Director: It's generally agreed that South is worth a raise to four hearts. But tactical considerations have to be borne in mind, and while the supporters of an immediate game raise are pleased with their virtue (I'm a simple soul who bids what he's got), the more crafty operators seem to have the edge in their arguments.

NUNES: 3♡. Little doubt that we can make game, but the vulnerability makes it likely that if I bid four the opponents will compete with four spades. I feel that three hearts will not be passed out and I will have a good chance of being 'forced' into four hearts. In fact, I would almost prefer to try my luck in five hearts, rather than defend against four spades.

BESSE: 3♡. The hand is worth ten tricks, but its competitive value is uncertain. By bidding three hearts only, South will hear what the other players have to say.

DORMER: 3♡. In competitive bidding I am by nature ingenuous to the point of oafishness, but a certain dissimulation is needed here. Partner will be on lead against a spade sacrifice and even if he *could* give me diamond ruffs he won't. Any diamond finesses are right for opponents and the hand cannot defend well for us.

Therefore we *must* corral the contract in hearts and, though South is obviously worth four on values, creepy-crawly tactics may be best. I'm not scared of being stranded in three hearts with a vulnerable game on. 170 or 200 is better than 100 from four spades doubled.

If you think you may want a diamond lead you can always bid the suit. So:

SHARPLES: 3◇. Quantitatively, of course, the hand is worth four hearts, but it would be premature and short-sighted to bid it directly. A diamond lead from partner, paving the way for a subsequent ruff, may well turn out to be a key play.

If you are going to bid a different suit at the three level there is something to be said for three clubs, I would have thought, but the Director did not agree.

A less savoury suggestion was to bid three clubs in order to let partner appraise the North–South prospects the better if East–West got too active in spades. But suppose this is passed out?

Unlikely.

P. S–D. provided his usual quaint conclusion:

SWINNERTON-DYER: 5♡. Normal expert theory is to underbid, hoping thereby to be allowed to play in four hearts. But I feel that this will not work here; and anyway, other policies demand at least a spokesman. Bid in this fashion, the hand will present East–West with a very nasty problem; and though I may not know what to do to four spades, I shall certainly double five.

An advance sacrifice, when vulnerable against not, is unexplored territory.

This was the marking:

CALL	AWARD	PANEL
3♡	10	6
4♡	9	6
3◇	7	2
3♣	5	2
5♡	4	1

You may note that, apart from the side-swipe in his opening remarks, the Director did not present the arguments of the group who voted four hearts. I was one of those and I don't know what I said at the time, but this is how I see it:

If you make one of the semi-bluff approach bids, such as three clubs, you give the opposition time to compare notes, as it were. Over three clubs West has six options: pass, double, three diamonds, three hearts, three spades, and four spades. If you go straight to four hearts, on the other hand, he has only three choices: pass, double, four spades. I think it's silly to give them room. They may well think that four hearts is an overbid, designed to drive them into a sacrifice. If they do bid four spades, then I will double and partner can make the final decision.

PART II
HOW HIGH SHALL WE GO?

8

Australian Bridge
Director: Keith McNeil

IMPs, N–S vul. You, South, hold:

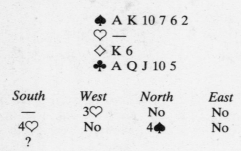

♠ A K 10 7 6 2
♡ —
♢ K 6
♣ A Q J 10 5

South	West	North	East
—	3♡	No	No
4♡	No	4♠	No
?			

You may not altogether agree with South's four hearts. I would prefer a cautious four spades myself. However, many of the panel took a very favourable view of the South hand. Not the first two, though.

ALDER: Pass. How disciplined or badly judged this call may be will depend on how it works out. Partner is expected (over four hearts) to make more than a minimum noise with anything that looks vaguely suitable for a slam.

MCCANCE: Pass. If there were enough values for a slam, North would be more helpful.

Director: The next panelist refutes this position.

MILES: 5♡. The risk of going down in five is less than the risk of missing a slam by passing. I couldn't expect partner to take strong action over four hearts (not even knowing what my suits are) with either

♠ J x x x ♡ x x x ◇ A x x x ♣ x x x

or

♠ Q x x x ♡ x x x x ◇ x x x ♣ K x x

Well, those are both 14-carders, as you may have noted. Blame it on the printers – we all do.

McNeil went on to quote three panelists who had pointed out that a slam could be on with as little as:

♠ x x x ♡ x x x ◇ x x x ♣ 9 x x x

They'd have to play it well, I must say.

BURGESS: 5♡. Cue-bid agreeing spades. North will be able to value his minor suit controls and trump length.

If he has either, yes.

CORNELL: 5♡. I would have liked to bid five spades, a more general-values type of move, but am afraid partner will look too closely at his spade suit missing at least two top honours.

McNeil agreed that the message of five spades would not be clear. Would five hearts be clearer? Two American panelists made an interesting point.

EISENBERG: 5♣. Must be forcing to five spades. With the ace of diamonds or the king of clubs, partner should bid the slam.
KANTAR: 5♣. Just guessing, but passing would also be a guess.

The point these two had in mind was that with a minor two-suiter South would have bid 4NT, not four hearts.

The man from Canada made a different point:

KEHELA: 5♡. Am tempted to make a slam try of six spades [joke], but East's silence is ominous.

Yes, indeed. Where are the rest of the hearts? With a limited hand including three or four hearts, East, especially at the score, would have made some move over three hearts. It is quite possible that North has more length in hearts than any other suit.

WOLFF: 5♠. Let partner make the first mistake.

One of the great comments (and practical, too)!

MAHMOOD: 6♠. Partner only needs to have four spades to make a good play for the slam.

CUMMINGS: 6♠. Five hearts, looking for seven, is an overstatement.

I agree with that, anyway.

SMITH: 6♠. Le punt.

This was the marking:

CALL	AWARD	PANEL
5♡	100	10
5♣	90	2
6♠	90	7
5♠	70	3
Pass	60	14

Never one to be browbeaten by his panel, McNeil explained that although the pass attracted the highest single number of votes, the majority opted for further action.

For my part, I agree with this comment:

COURTNEY: Pass. The partnership's first duty over a pre-empt is to get to a sound game.

There are two hazards in this kind of situation. One is that the adverse distribution, after the pre-empt, may be horrific; the other is that bids that seem innocent on paper, such as five hearts or five clubs in this instance, *may* be misunderstood. It happens!

9

Bridge Magazine
Director: Eric Milnes

IMPs, both vul. You, South, hold:

♠ A
♡ K Q 6 3 2
♢ K 8 6 4
♣ Q 10 2

South	West	North	East
—	—	No	1♡
No	1NT	2♣	No
?			

Director: Another action v. non-action situation. Although the pass gets more votes than any other bid there is an eleven to six majority in favour of doing something. I therefore give top marks to the positive bid with most support.

These situations where everyone else is bidding and you suspect that you have the best hand at the table are often difficult. Is there a fair chance of a game your way? If so, will it be in notrumps or in spades? Not much doubt about that, I would have said, but two good bidders approach the problem with a bid in notrumps.

SHARPLES: 2NT. A little deficient to insist on game. 2NT does not rule out a spade contract, but to give immediate spade support certainly rules out notrumps, and this could easily be best.

How easily? You know what these hands are like when you have a singleton ace of partner's long suit.

MARX: 2NT. It is quite likely that North will not favour notrumps and will be inclined to attempt a suit contract, either in spades or some other. North's vulnerable overcall will not in itself guarantee the values for game, but the strong encouraging response of 2NT leaves all the options open.

Including, I would have thought, the option of partner passing 2NT, which won't play at all well. East has opened the bidding, vulnerable, West has responded 1NT, and you hold 14 points. There are only about 7 or 8 points left for North, and if he has bid two spades on something like ♠ K J 10 8 x x and a king, surely he may withdraw before worse befalls? Also, if North does retreat to three spades, what will South do next?

Several panelists thought it more sensible to raise the spades, as proposed by:

AUHAGEN: 3♠. Very difficult to judge. Partner cannot have many points. His suit, therefore, must be very good. Game is worth trying. Maybe a bold leap to four would spare partner a headache.

Sparing partner a headache:

FOX: 4♠. With South holding so many points, North's overcall must be based on a good suit as he has not much else.

Then there were the cautious ones who were going to make sure of a plus score.

PIGOT: Pass. I expect he'll make nine tricks, but I can't see ten.
MOLLO: Pass. I have the right things in the wrong places.

This was an accurate and, I dare say, a shrewd remark.

This was the marking:

CALL	AWARD	PANEL
2NT	10	4
3♠	9	4
4♠	8	2
Pass	7	6
3♡	2	1

30

More credit might have been given to Besse's three hearts, which I suppose was a way of saying 'I am worth at least three spades – bid four if you can.'

I was among the three-spade bidders at the time, but it may be that this is more of a panelist's answer than a realistic one. The man is going to pass three spades, you know that. So you may as well let him play in two spades, prepared to take the blame if he makes ten tricks.

10

Bridge International
Director: Keith McNeil

IMPs, N–S vul. You, South, hold:

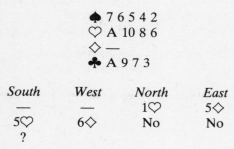

♠ 7 6 5 4 2
♡ A 10 8 6
♢ —
♣ A 9 7 3

South	West	North	East
—	—	1♡	5♢
5♡	6♢	No	No
?			

There are only two possibilities – six hearts or double – and two main points to consider. (1) Is North's pass over six diamonds a firm encouragement to bid on? And (2) on a simple question of valuation, are you worth an advance to six hearts?

McNeil, generally quite willing to put his distinguished panel in its place, seemed to be somewhat uncertain about this one. We shall go straight into the panel's answers therefore, looking first at those who felt impelled to take positive action.

FORRESTER: 6♡. If North can make a forcing pass and I hold two aces, then surely six hearts must be near. At least half the time they'll save anyway, so I'll gain 5 IMP.

I'm not so sure about that. Most players, nowadays, are reluctant to be pushed into a sacrifice that may be a phantom. East–West will have noted that you bid only five hearts first time round.

GAROZZO: 6♡. My partner's pass is forcing, proposing to play six if my hand is suitable.

Yes, but is it suitable?

MOLLO: 6♡. After partner's forcing pass my only fear is of missing a grand slam.

There were those who did not value the South hand so highly.

ALDER: Double. In my book partner's pass is forcing, but I think it unlikely he can make six opposite this. My suits have no fillers, just three first-round controls – and one of these might be duplicated in partner's hand.

HIRON: Double. I doubt whether North's pass is forcing (though a case can be made), but my five hearts was feeble in the extreme. Another disaster, I dare say.

What's he talking about? If five hearts was feeble, why is he not bidding six now? (Perhaps he had one or two libations between the first part of the answer and the second?)

REESE: Double. You were stretching when you bid five hearts, were you not?

The old pessimist again, some will say. Much depends on partner's spade holding. If he has a singleton the hands may go well together, but if has something like A J x there will be insuperable losers.

ROWLANDS: Double. Tempting to press on after partner's pass, but I could have had much more for my five heart bid.

KANTAR: Double. With both of us short of diamonds, I don't like our chances of making six hearts. Against certain opponents it would surely be right to bid six hearts as they would automatically bid seven diamonds.

As I said above, I don't think that's a safe assumption. Opponents know you bid only five hearts first time round.

In case you are changing your opinion, I will conclude with one or two more of the six-heart supporters.

WOLFF: 6♡. This may even be a save.

A timid wolf.

33

SHARPLES: 6♡. Difficult to know in this free-for-all who expects to make what, but in view of the vulnerability and partner's pass I'll chance six hearts, but will be happier if they go on to seven diamonds.

Director: Well, there it is – both arguments are very cogent, but the chance of non-vulnerable opponents taking the save seems to me to give the six-hearters a slight edge.

This was the marking:

CALL	AWARD	PANEL
6♡	10	12
Double	8	9

Let's look again at the two questions posed at the beginning of this discussion. First, is North's pass over six diamonds a firm encouragement to bid six hearts?

I think it is right to say that if North had a balanced minimum he would double. He might also, for tactical reasons, pass, intending to go to six hearts if you (South) double. (*Of course* the pass is forcing: you are not going to let the defending side play at slam level undoubled.) But if North is open-minded, he may still pass. He is not, as Garozzo implies, pressing you to bid six hearts.

Second, if North does not bid six hearts (as he still may after you have doubled), do you expect to make twelve tricks? There are thousands of hands that would provide a good play for the slam, and still more that wouldn't. At least, that's how I see it. Those empty black suits could so easily contain two losers.

11

Bridge International
Director: Bill Pencharz

IMPs, none vul. You, South, hold:

♠ Q 6 4 3
♡ K 4
◇ Q J 3 2
♣ J 6 4

South	West	North	East
No	No	1♣	No
1◇	No	3◇	No
?			

For most players (one or two exceptions will appear later) the question will be whether to pass or bid 3NT.

Director: This hand turned up in Shanghai, where it was held by Robert Sheehan against one of China's Vice-Premiers. Sheehan bid 3NT and made it against a poor defence. Incidentally, the North hand held by Irving Rose was ♠ A K 9 ♡ 7 3 ◇ K 9 8 4 ♣ A Q 3 2. Observe how, in standard Rose–Sheehan style, Rose opened this hand one club. If such is the way of modern bidding, I would rather play the banjo.

And I'm sure you would be very good at it. To open one club is ancient as well as modern; further comment later on.

Meanwhile:

SHEEHAN: Pass. The defence is likely to be ahead of you in one of the majors before you can set up nine tricks.

ALDER: (remembering): Pass. If Sheehan says pass, I pass! However, I fancy the majority will be tempted to proceed, not noticing the nine-plus losers.

This was good prophecy.

LAVINGS: 3NT. Stoppers in both majors, notrump cards, a 9-count – what could be more ideal?

MCNEIL: 3NT. Ever an optimist. Pass is possibly right, but I know I'd never achieve it at the table.

SCHROEDER: 3NT. He has promised me something like 16–18 high-card points with five clubs and four diamonds. What do you want to play in other than 3NT?

Will North be as heavy as that? I doubt it. There may be some borderline hands, but in general the sequence suggests 4–6 and about 14–16 points. With a strong 1–2–4–6 it should be safe, especially with a passed partner, to jump-shift in the doubleton major and then advance with minimum steps in the minors.

The passers had rather more to say.

SOLOWAY: Pass. Game is not cold opposite a hand with 14–16 high-card points. If partner has more high cards and less distribution, 3NT will have a good play, but it is anti-percentage to stretch for a non-vulnerable game.

SHARPLES: Pass. To bid any game here is likely to result in a minus score. Partner, for example, doesn't have to hold more than about 14 points with a likely 1–3–4–5 distribution.

If he has only 14 points I think he is more likely to be 1–2–4–6. With 1–3–4–5 one tends to hold back a little, expecting partner to be able to bid again over two diamonds.

The oddities were 5♢ by Besse, presumably in support of my idea that North's 3♢ is distributional, and:

JOURDAIN: 3♡. Partner is likely to have a singleton in one of the majors, so 3NT is premature.

Will it become less premature after 3♡? It will become silly if partner, with x x in hearts, thinks *he* can bid 3NT. Giving the women the last say:

KENNEDY (Betty Ann): 3NT. Five or six club tricks, two or three diamonds, and a trick on the lead, add up to nine (I hope).

PRIDAY (Jane): Pass. Anyone who finds another call on this collection is either (a) a beginner, or (b) trying for a swing, or (c) drunk.

This was the marking:

CALL	AWARD	PANEL
3NT	10	17
Pass	6	7
3♡	3	1
5◇	2	1

I suppose this problem really depends on how one interprets the raise to three diamonds. My view is that it is likely to be shapely, not an encouragement to 3NT. I agree with Soloway's comment.

Going back to the opening bid on the 3–2–4–4 type held by Rose, Pencharz declares: *When 4–4 in the minors one opens a diamond.* In a footnote Alder, who was editor at the time, commented that an opening one club left better chances to find a fit in either minor. That is true, and in any case I think it is wrong to decide in advance how you will handle any particular distribution. Quality of the suits is important, too.

12

Bridge Magazine
Director: Eric Milnes

Pairs, both vul. You, South, hold:

♠ Q 10 9 7
♡ K
♢ J 5
♣ A Q J 8 5 3

South	West	North	East
—	1♣	1♡	No
?			

The problems on this occasion were set by Alan Hiron, but the feature was presented by the Director, Eric Milnes. He made only one comment:

If ever there was a time for sitting back, this is it. Pass, and start to sharpen your little axe.

Some panelists counted their 13 points, noting the good intermediates in spades, and took the offensive in one way or another.

AUHAGEN: 2♣. The cheapest bid available. Maybe partner is able to introduce spades as second suit. After two hearts I shall pass and over two diamonds I would bid 2NT.

MARX: 2♣. Thirteen points, even though imperfectly fitting, cannot be ignored after a vulnerable bid from partner. 1NT is scarcely adequate, and the more encouraging cue-bid does not commit the side to game. In fact, if all partner can do is to repeat himself with two hearts, South would be best advised to pass.

Blowing hot, then cold.

PIGOT: 2♣ . . . to be going on with. No point rushing into notrumps until a clearer picture is available.

NORTH: 1♠. A difficult bid. Ideally one should have five spades, but we have a certain amount of compensation in other places. Perhaps one should not overlook the fact that there is nothing in the rules to prevent partner holding four spades himself.

But still, players with 4–5 in the major suits generally employ a special type of overcall.

Other panelists were very much aware of the disadvantages in the South hand: the singleton king of hearts and the fact that clubs had been bid on the left.

MOLLO: Pass. North would have doubled if he had something in spades as well as hearts. In notrumps we might have serious communication problems.

AMSBURY: Pass. When in doubt I always aim for a plus score at pairs. There may be a game, but we may also have to deal with diamond bids by partner if we proceed.

ROWLANDS: 1NT. Ugh – I probably should pass but in case partner is good I will give him a chance.

REESE: 1NT. All you can do at present. What game do you expect to make with no communications and your good suit called on your left?

This was the marking:

CALL	AWARD	PANEL
1NT	10	6
Pass	8	3
2♣	6	4
1♠	3	2
2NT	4	1

The optimist who recommended 2NT was Tony Trad. Perhaps their standard for vulnerable overcalls is (or was) fairly high in Switzerland.

This is going to be an awkward hand in the play whichever side obtains the contract, and it may be that in the modern world, at any rate, a pass is the best tactical move. I say 'in the modern world', because the fashion nowadays is for the responder to pass on many fair hands and for the first player to reopen. If opponents do this, you may well catch them for a penalty. An interesting situation would arise if the bidding were to develop like this:

South	West	North	East
—	1♣	1♡	No
No	dble	No	2♢
?			

It would be premature to double two diamonds. I like two hearts at this point, on the singleton king. An opponent with x x x in hearts may think his partner is short and may go to three diamonds. Certainly you can double this.

13

Bridge International
Director: Eric Crowhurst

IMPs, both vul. You, South, hold:

♠ Q 10 2
♥ A K 9 6 5
♦ 4
♣ A Q 8 3

South	West	North	East
—	—	1♦	No
1♥	No	4♥	No
5♣	No	5♦	No
?			

Are you almost in grand slam territory or are you to allow for the possibility that partner may hold two losing spades? The Director began:

The decision whether or not to proceed beyond five hearts in this situation centres on our view of partner's likely holding in the critical spade suit. A number of panelists believe that partner is unlikely to hold the spade ace.

FORRESTER: 6♥. With a spade control and a good raise, partner would bid three spades and not four hearts, so I don't think seven is possible.

His point is that if North had held such as ♠ A x ♥ Q J x x ♦ A K Q x x ♣ K x he would have made a conventional bid – either three spades or some sort of reverse Swiss (4♣ or 4♦). Similarly:

SHARPLES: 6♡. With other stronger bids available, the jump to four hearts usually signifies a hand with a lack of primary controls.

JOURDAIN: 6♡. Although it is just possible that partner has two losing spades, it is highly unlikely and we should be prepared to bid the slam on general values.

I am perfectly happy to go along with that. I do not accept, however, that partner has absolutely guaranteed a spade control by cue-bidding five diamonds.

There is disagreement on this point:

SOLOWAY: 6♡. If partner bid four hearts on a hand containing two losing spades, I don't think he should cue-bid over five clubs.

PARRY: 6♡. Although it is a matter of style, I expect partner to control spades when he bids five diamonds.

Why should this be? Crowhurst demands, enlisting a fair amount of support.

ROWLANDS: 5♡. I wouldn't have bid like this, but having decided to be scientific and pinpoint my weakness, I can hardly bid a slam with no spade control.

HAUSLER: 5♡. As North cannot hold first-round spade control after his bid of four hearts, he is now called upon to bid the slam with second-round control.

The implication of this remark is that you cannot follow a sequence such as 1◇–1♡–4♡ when (as opener) you hold the ace of spades. Such an understanding might be useful on occasion, but it is certainly not universal.

PRIDAY (Jane): 5♡. Judging by partner's bidding, it is unlikely that he holds two small spades, but it is a possibility. Anyway, I'm not going to bid the slam for him. He will know from my five hearts that I'm asking for first or second-round control of spades, and he will bid five spades with the ace or six hearts with the king or singleton.

I could not have put it better myself.

Funny, because I think the five-heart bidders are missing a clear inference. If South, after 1♢–1♡–4♡, holds a control in spades he must (if intending to bid on) show it. *Therefore*, when North invites a slam by bidding five diamonds over five clubs, he *guarantees* that he does not hold two losers in spades. Think it out. Anyway, just look at the South hand: it is ridiculous not to accept the slam invitation conveyed by five diamonds.

This was the marking:

CALL	AWARD	PANEL
5♡	10	10
6♡	9	9
6♢	6	1
5NT	3	2

If my contention that North must hold a spade control is right, the question arises whether South should suggest a grand slam with 5NT. That is more doubtful, because even if North held the ace of spades you might need a finesse, or a good break in diamonds, for seven.

14

IPBM

Directors: Joe Amsbury and Brian Senior

IMPs, none vul. You, South, hold:

♠ 10 7 4 2
♡ K J 9 8
♢ A Q 10
♣ J 10

South	West	North	East
—	—	1♣	No
1♡	No	1♠	No
?			

This may seem a rather pedestrian affair, but some interesting points arose from the answers. Amsbury, for one, had no doubt about the best action.

Pedants raise spades. Practical bidders go for the 'obvious' notrumps. If they count this as 11 points (2NT), they don't count.

He had support from:

KLINGER: 3NT. Natural, not forcing. Look at all those intermediates. (Second choice, 2NT, natural, not forcing.)

PRICE: 3NT. Despite a mere 11 points this hand is worth game and the texture is best suited to notrumps. Hence 3NT, which partner is allowed to pull if 5–5 in the blacks.

REBATTU: 3NT. With good fitting cards and stoppers I am too strong for 2NT. If partner is not interested in notrumps I may still retreat to four spades after four clubs or four diamonds.

What say the pedants?

ARMSTRONG: 3♠. Although my red suits are very strong I still prefer spades to notrumps.

So you say, but why?

FLINT: 3♠. A problem for the Lower Fourth.

This puzzled me, and I tested him with the same question a year or two later. The reply: '2NT'.

LANDY (Sandra): 3♠. Do you want me to bid 2NT? My partner has five clubs and four spades when she bids like this and I want to play in spades even if it is wrong.

ROWLANDS: 3♠. No doubt 2NT might work better. At least I won't upset pard if I am wrong this way, but a 2NT bid, if three spades would have worked better, is likely to disrupt partnership confidence.

PALOOKA: 3♠. Losing Trick Count, and all that. I don't believe, as the adjudicator will tell you, in confusing the game of bridge by thinking.

A mixture, for sure. Contempt, obstinacy, cowardice and ignorance the claimed reasons.

FORRESTER: 2♢. Caught between a desire to bid three spades and 2NT, I will hedge my bets. If he bids 2NT I pass (as we are non-vulnerable); over three clubs I will bid 3NT; and I will bid two spades over two hearts. I am not keen on the spade fit.

LODGE: 2♢. Playing IMPs and with all these intermediates I am going to game, but where? Perhaps when the 'problem' reaches a stage where we actually have a problem, we shall see!

Expressing my view:

REESE: 2NT. Looks more like this than a raise to three spades, and you can throw 'two diamonds' into the dustbin.

This bitter remark about two diamonds was exaggerated: the bid won't stop you arriving in 3NT.

YOUNG: 2NT. A very interesting problem. Three spades looked right at first, but with only 1 point in partner's suits, and with such good red-suit holdings, 2NT must be the better bet.

KEHELA: 2NT. Or as I say, two without. Without good spades. ('Two without' is the continental way of saying two notrumps.)

Kokish and Sharples both voted for 2NT, remarking that 3NT would not be wrong. Also:

SOLOWAY: 2NT. This looks like a notrump hand with my black-suit holdings.

Still think it is an underbid.

This was the marking.

CALL	AWARD	PANEL
2NT	10	9
3NT	8	4
3♠	7	6
2◇	6	2

I think, on reflection, that 3NT is right. It is the sort of hand on which, playing in 2NT, you make ten tricks. One point that no one mentioned is that after this kind of auction the defenders often lead the major suit that has not been supported – a spade in this case.

15

Bridge International
Director: Hugh Kelsey

IMPs, N–S vul. You, South, hold:

♠ Q 3
♡ 4
♢ A Q 10 7 6 3
♣ Q 10 4 2

South	West	North	East
—	1♡	dble	1♠
3♢	3♡	No	4♡
?			

There are five possibilities here – pass, double, 4NT, 5♣, 5♢ – and all had supporters. The most popular, in this field of experienced bidders, was:

BENJAMIN: 4NT. Three diamonds was limited, so 4NT shows 6–4 in the minors.

FORRESTER: 4NT. I was worth more than three diamonds last time, so 4NT is hardly an overbid. The panel will probably double, but I'm not sure that's best. Eleven tricks may be easier than four.

Director: Only two doubled, which seems to indicate that your bidding is better than your forecasting.

It is perhaps a little strange that only two doubled. These were Hiron and Mollo, and their observations were not quoted.

LEV: 4NT. Shows six diamonds and four clubs. With 6–5 or 5–5 distribution I would bid five clubs, not 4NT.

ROHAN: 4NT. Shows good diamonds and a lesser club suit. Even if we cannot make eleven tricks, the opponents are likely to go to five hearts at this vulnerability.

I wouldn't be too sure of that. The opponents are likely to reflect that you bid only three diamonds on the previous round but are now competing at the five level.

4NT seems better than five clubs, but this had its supporters, too.

COHN: 5♣. Six would be a bit much.

We may hate your bid, but it is very unlikely that anyone will quarrel with your comment.

MCNEIL: 5♣. East may be 'operating' with his one-spade response. We must have a fit somewhere (maybe partner will have one when he sees my hand).

Witty and wise; it's almost too much.

NORTH: 5♣. Since there is every prospect of landing a game that depends on no more than a finesse, we should surely bid it. Maybe this is not the right action for widows, orphans and those of a nervous disposition. Looks okay for the remainder.

SOLOWAY: 5♣. I should have cue-bid to start with. Now I'm just guessing. The right fit will easily make game.

One panelist stuck to his guns.

MESBUR: 5♢. Confidently.

What (since the time when he bid a non-forcing three diamonds) has happened to make him so confident of five?

And there were some nervous folk who passed.

BESSE: Pass. If North didn't find a bid after South's jump, then South in turn has no more to say.

HAUSLER: Pass. At favourable vulnerability I might try 4NT, but it is too speculative.

48

LAVINGS: Pass. To bid the one-off five diamonds must be wrong. Nor do I have a double. Perhaps partner has some thoughts?

REESE: Pass. The defensive chances are too good for you to try 4NT.

SHARPLES: Pass. Too high for further action. A double is not attractive either.

WOLFF: Pass. Whatever could we bid now?

Eighteen panelists managed to think of something.

This was the marking:

CALL	AWARD	PANEL
4NT	10	10
5♣	7	5
Pass	6	7
5♢	3	3
Double	2	2

Usually, when I look at a problem after an interval, I can be convinced, or nearly, by the answer I gave before, but not on this occasion. To pass is feeble, really. There is no assurance that partner will be able to bid over four hearts.

What of the others? Five clubs and 4NT really amount to the same thing. Will you ever gain from playing in clubs? I doubt it.

Five diamonds might be right, but I feel that Double was underestimated by the panel. Partner is still there, remember. What you are telling him is that, in addition to long diamonds, you have some high cards. It will still be open to him to bid five diamonds (or something else). If he passes, and they make four hearts, I shall tell him to brush up his take-out doubles.

16

IPBM

Director: Joe Amsbury

IMPs, none vul. You, South, hold:

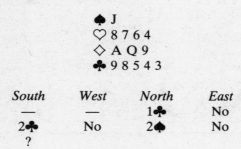

♠ J
♡ 8 7 6 4
♢ A Q 9
♣ 9 8 5 4 3

South	West	North	East
—	—	1♣	No
2♣	No	2♠	No
?			

This, in fact, was the second part of a two-part question. The first part concerned South's response to the opening one club. Do you see any sort of sensible alternative to two clubs? Nor do I, but there was what they call a 'substantial minority' for one heart.

Let us pass from that to the present question. You have a little in hand, obviously, after the simple raise, and this prompted some panelists to jump over the gate.

KLINGER: 4♢. Cue-bid, promising short spades and the diamond ace.

Why it should promise short spades, I don't know.

ROWLANDS: 5♣. With a super-suitable hand, the least I can do is say so, loud and clear.

REBATTU: 2NT. I shall propose a 3NT contract. If partner retreats to three clubs I will make a try for five clubs.

PALOOKA: 2NT. This shows that I am not as terrible as I might be. I have – after all – bid two clubs on the first round, so partner will not expect much more.

Show plus values, but why not show where they are?

WERDELIN: 3◇. Accepting the game try but undecided about the final contract.

SOLOWAY: 3◇. Good values for a two-clubs raise. Will pass four clubs now, as three diamonds shows extras.

More optimistic:

PRICE: 3◇. I am going to game at least and would like to describe where my values are. 3NT may be best, but if partner is 5–1–2–5 a slam may be on.

FORRESTER: 3◇. Surely not a problem now. My two-club response has worked well.

COLLINGS: 3◇. For two reasons: my values are there for notrumps and I also have good reserves. Perhaps even six clubs if partner has:

♠ A K x x ♡ x ◇ K x x ♣ A K x x x

Perhaps; the sun does shine occasionally.

This was the marking:

CALL	AWARD	PANEL
3◇	10	15
4◇	7	1
2NT	5	3
5♣	4	1

This was a high vote for a good bid that is not all that obvious; in an event of average standard the majority would bid 2NT, would they not? If you bid this you will certainly miss the occasional slam that may be on. Responses such as four diamonds or five clubs may turn out all right – probably will – but these bids leave 3NT out of the reckoning.

17

Australian Bridge
Director: Keith McNeil

IMPs, N–S vul. You, South, hold:

♠ A Q 8 6 5
♡ 10
◇ K 10 9 3 2
♣ A 6

South	West	North	East
—	—	—	No
1♠	2♡	2♠	3♡
?			

McNeil did not think highly – and I agree with him – of four panelists who did not think the hand worth more than three spades.

CUMMINGS: 3♠. Inviting the game.

CUPPAIDGE: 3♠. Unequivocally invitational. The hand does not justify a direct four spades, especially as partner very likely has values in hearts.

This was one of the most peculiar comments I have ever heard. McNeil was surprisingly tolerant, saying only:

Why? He may have some sort of length, but the odds are two to one that the opponents have most of the heart points.

ROTH: 3♠. Can't afford to jump to game or bid four diamonds.

SWANSON: 3♠. I do not believe that this is the type of sequence to blast into game on the premise that West will be bludgeoned into a save.

I must confess that the only reason I would ever find this astounding underbid is the old tactical ploy of hoping to be pushed into four spades and being allowed to play there peacefully.

There were several supporters for four diamonds:

BOARDMAN: 4◇. Long suit, informative and helping partner if there is further competition.

BURGESS: 4◇. North will now be in a position to judge the best action if the opponents bid five hearts.

I trust he will double or pass and let me double.

The majority were for four spades:

MAHMOOD: 4♠. Hoping to buy the contract. The alternative, four diamonds, would allow partner to be better placed, but I don't really want to play five spades after a two-spade response.

GILL: 4♠. With the five-loser hand four spades appeals, not four diamonds because I do not want to encourage partner to bid five spades over five hearts at this vulnerability.

REESE: 4♠. Let them do the guessing. Don't give West a chance to bid four hearts.

Another excellent point in favour of four spades, says McNeil of the next comment:

SEBESFI: 4♠. I would rather overbid a 5–5, once a suit has been supported, than underbid it.

There were supporters, also, for a competitive double of three hearts, for the reason expressed in the following answers.

SOLOWAY: Double. A game try in spades. Three spades would be competitive [i.e. not inviting a raise to game].

FORQUET: Double. In my language it means three-and-a-half spades since three spades is only competitive.

CORNELL: Double. Obviously I was going to make a game try in diamonds. Over three hearts this seems best now.

A novel suggestion commended itself to the Director.

KLINGER: 4♣. A psychic long-suit trial bid in order to persuade the opponents that they have some defence when four spades is ultimately bid.

Confession time! I must be as devious as Klinger – I like it! Hence the promotion. (In the marking, he means.) *Finally:*

MOSES: 4♠. (It is this panelist's practice to add a little rhyme or quotation. This time he ended:

> But at my back I always hear
> Tim's words of wisdom in my ear:
> Bid your limit – no delay,
> That's where you're going anyway!)

Tim being Tim Seres, ex-Hungarian grandmaster of Australian bridge.

This was the marking:

CALL	AWARD	PANEL
4♠	100	15
4♣	80	1
4◇	80	12
Dble	70	4
3♠	40	4

The advantage of four spades, as I see it, is that it forces the opponents to make their decision at a high level. If you adopt any of the alternatives you give them a chance to make another call below the level of four spades, and this may help them to do the right thing later.

18

IPBM

Director: Joe Amsbury

IMPs, N–S vul. You, South, hold:

♠ Q 7 5 2
♡ K J 10 5
♢ 10 6 5
♣ A 5

South	West	North	East
No	No	1♠	3♣
?			

East's three clubs is described as weak.

Most of the problems in this book have struck me as – problems. This one doesn't. Not in a hundred years would it have occurred to me to include it in a bidding competition.

Imagine that the bidding had begun: 1♠ – pass – ? It is a sound raise to three spades, some would say to four spades. On the present occasion (a) you have passed originally, and (b) East has come in with three clubs. Let us consider first the effect of East's three clubs: Does this improve your hand or not? I would say not, for two reasons: The ace of clubs loses value – it will be worth just one playing trick (normally an ace is worth nearly two in the end); and there is the danger of unbalanced distribution – perhaps a singleton heart will be led, perhaps the trumps will be awkward.

So far, therefore, the hand is certainly not improved. What about the fact that you have passed originally? Does that make your hand any better? No, it does not, and there is the further consideration that partner is third in hand.

The South hand looks to me the plainest, most ordinary, least disputable raise to three spades in the history of the game. Now see how it struck the others.

Director: The general point for debate here is that, especially having passed, a 3♠ bid could be just a competitive gesture. I'll go along with that – at IMPs – but having passed, can 4♣ ever be misread?

Of course it can be misread. The bid does not mean: 'I can just scrape up a raise to game and among my values is the ace of clubs.' It means: 'Although I passed originally, the club intervention has improved my hand and there may even be a slam in spades.'

But Amsbury had his supporters:

LODGE: 4♣. I can't be any better than this. Will bid 4♡ over 4◇ given the chance.

And, I suppose, the old Black over four spades.

SILVER:4♠. This is an overbid, but 3♠ in competition can be bid with a lot less than I actually have. In effect, 4♠ is less of an overbid than 3♠ is an underbid.

KOKISH: Double. Then 3♠ over three of a red suit. But maybe I should just drive it via 4♣ or 4◇.

PENCHARZ: 4♠. Must take the pressure off partner. Anyone who doubles (sputnik) must be a descendant of the late and unlamented Nero.

PRICE: Double. Worth a double before supporting spades (which I would do at the four level) just in case partner has hearts. For example, 6♡ is good opposite:

♠ A K x x x x   ♡ A Q x x   ◇ x   ♣ x x

And you expect to finish in six hearts? That's what the lawyers call special pleading.

COLLINGS: 4♠. I don't like dragging up a 3♠ bid.

Some don't mind:

FORRESTER: 3♠. Yes, I know I'm under pressure, but to bid 4♠ opposite a third-in-hand opener is sadistic (and masochistic). This is dead-centre for 1♠ – 3♠, so why distort it? In fact, why set the problem in the first place?

BROCK: 3♠. What I always had to bid. I must be overlooking some clever answer – perhaps all the finesses are right.

Looks more and more correct to bid 4♠, for gain if partner's good and strain if he's weak. By the way, game was cold and North was minimum. This was the last hand of the European Championship in the ladies' match between GB and Sweden. If our girl had bid only 3♠, they would not be going to Brazil.

I saw the North hand somewhere and my recollection is that she had enough to go to four spades. This was the marking:

CALL	AWARD	PANEL
3♠	10	13
4♣	9	1
4♠	8	9
Double	5	3

Many panelists seem to take the view that a raise to three spades would be 'competitive' and below normal standards. I don't see why, especially in the modern climate where the opener is very ready to reopen with a double. Steve Lodge, it seems to me, was handsomely rewarded for his singular choice of four clubs.

PART III
THAT'S A BIT AWKWARD!

19

British Bridge World
Director: Alan Truscott

Rubber bridge, none vul. You, South, hold:

> ♠ 9 5 3 2
> ♡ A J 3
> ◇ A Q 6
> ♣ 8 3 2

South	West	North	East
—	1♣	dble	No
?			

Director: All the panelists found this an 'impossible' bid and were concerned to find the least evil. (Least evil solution, that is.)

SMART: 2NT. A vile bid, but anything else seems viler.

REESE: 2NT. Nothing else presents itself. If partner raises on a singleton or doubleton honour, spades may be blocked or may not be led.

There was perhaps a slight edge to the Director's note: *This practical comment reveals an attribute which not all our leading performers possess: willingness to adopt what is believed to be the right bid without regard for the reactions of partner, team-mates or critics if a silly result is obtained.*

Others cling to the idea that a guard in the enemy suit is useful for notrumps.

NUNES: 2♣. It is the thing to bid some number of notrumps, but I will look foolish if partner has no spade boost and five or six spades are run against me.

FILARSKI: 2♠. Perhaps a dangerous bid, for after 2♠ – 3◇ – 4◇ the contract may go too high; and after 2♠ – 3♣ South is in difficulties. But I would rather play in five diamonds than in 1NT.

Truscott himself favoured the tactical underbid of 1NT: *Although there is a clear majority for aggressive action, a sound case can be made for the massive underbid of 1NT. This is very much the type of hand on which the values for game are present but no game can be made.* (This view had some support.)

PHILLIPS: 1NT. The objection to bidding two spades is that there will then be almost no chance to stay short of game. 1NT is an underbid, admittedly; we can only pray that partner will speak again.

Such prayers are seldom answered in these situations.

There was an original suggestion from Yorkshire:

HOCHWALD: 2◇. Very, very difficult. Two spades is unsatisfactory – what do I do if partner then bids three clubs? A notrump response may lead to a hopeless 3NT. I cannot find a bid which describes the hand, so I bid two diamonds and wait for further developments. It is unlikely that this bid will be passed.

What optimists these Yorkshiremen are! I would not mind betting my brand new conductor's baton to one local point (in the master-point scheme) that there ain't going to be any further developments.

This was the marking:

CALL	AWARD	PANEL
2♠	10	4
2NT	10	4
1NT	7	3
2◇	1	2

Unless you revert to the early Culbertson theory that a response of 1NT to a double always shows values, there is no good answer to this problem. The objection that Phillips raises to two spades seems a sound one: you cannot die on the next round and so can hardly stay short of game.

If you are going to look for a 'funny' bid, then surely two hearts would be better than Hochwald's two diamonds. Partner might raise hearts where, with similar values, he would pass two diamonds. He might even hold five hearts and not be able to introduce them over two diamonds. I am thinking of a hand such as:

♠ x   ♡ K 10 x x x   ♢ K J x   ♣ A J 10 x

But let's face it, there is no answer that will work well more than half the time.

20

British Bridge World
Director: Alan Hiron

IMPs, none vul. You, South, hold:

♠ Q
♡ 9 7 3 2
♢ A 8 6 5
♣ A J 7 4

South	West	North	East
—	—	No	No
No	1♠	dble	3♠
?			

North–South are playing responsive doubles up to three hearts only.

There is a 'bright' answer to this problem, but let's look at some of the others first.

RODRIGUE: 4♡. Partner's double of one spade after passing must guarantee four hearts. Quite possibly the limit of the hand is nine tricks for either side, but let's leave the opposition to guess. For my part, I'm prepared to double four spades if they bid it.

MRS MARKUS: 4♡; and if the opponents bid four spades I shall try 4NT.

You will? Your partner did pass originally, you know.

COLLINGS: 4♡. This should not go more than one down, even if doubled, but more likely we shall collect 300 from four spades doubled.

RIMINGTON: Pass. A gift. Even the panel won't contest at the four level at equal vulnerability with a passed partner. Now prove me wrong.

It may well be that neither side can make a game, but if you pass three spades, so will they.

Director: And the last little piggy was so cross at not being allowed to play 'a well integrated system with responsive doubles' that he said:

BARBOUR: 4♠. It is more important to play in the right suit than at the right level on these hands.

Maybe, but there was a better answer, supported by exactly half the panel.

CROWHURST: 3NT. If the hearts were better, of course, there would be no need for buck passing.

REESE: 3NT. I had this position in Beirut (European Championship) and my indolent partner passed with nothing in spades. I think that 3NT is more useful as a take-out than to show, for example, a spade stop and a long minor suit.

BESSE: 3NT. Clearly a take-out. South's hand justifies competition at the four level at least.

SMART: 3NT. Practically inconceivable that this can be misinterpreted.

Ha!

The popular 3NT seems logical, as it must be for take-out after both partners have passed. True, it might be construed as showing minor suits only, and this persuaded some to introduce the dubious heart suit; a doubtful move.

This was the marking:

CALL	AWARD	PANEL
3NT	10	9
4♡	8	5
Pass	5	2
4♣	2	1
4♠	2	1

4–4–4–1 hands are particularly unpromising when, as here, partner is likely to be short in the same suit as you are. It is unlikely that your side can make four hearts – remember that partner passed originally – and if the suit is divided 4–1 you will be doubled for ever after. It is certainly more prudent to name a minor suit at the four level. If they go to four spades, double with a clear conscience.

21

IPBM

Director: Joe Amsbury

IMPs, none vul. You, South, hold:

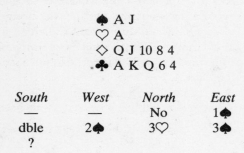

♠ A J
♡ A
♢ Q J 10 8 4
♣ A K Q 6 4

South	West	North	East
—	—	No	1♠
dble	2♠	3♡	3♠
?			

You wouldn't have doubled one spade? You may say that now, but it is a difficult hand to manage. Would you have overcalled with an unusual 2NT? Unusual, indeed, with 21 points, and this too would be difficult to follow up. So, let's consider what to do as the bidding has gone.

COLLINGS: 3NT. And pray. Four diamonds is my next choice, to be followed by five clubs if given the chance. One factor is that partner should have a suit and not some scattered values which he could have shown via a responsive double.

What 'scattered values' can he have? There is not room for him to hold more than three or four points, and the odds are that these will all be in hearts.

WERDELIN: 3NT. I cannot claim that 3NT is without risk, but compared with the alternatives it should be safer and aims at the most probable game for us.

Director: That's the total vote for what I mentally chose when watching.

Quite enough, too. I can think of only about one plausible holding that would give you a play for game in no trumps: credit North with 10 x x of spades and king of diamonds.

There was support for four clubs.

KELSEY: 4♣. Offering the choice of minor suits. If North persists with four hearts, that is likely to be the right spot.

FORRESTER: 4♣. There are three possible courses of action and all have merit. Double – the contract should go off unless partner has club length; too chancy. 3NT – a sensible partner should realize that if I had a spade guard and a solid minor I would have bid 3NT over one spade. Four clubs; as there is a lot of distribution about, North is more likely to have a second suit.

KANTAR: 4◇. Planning to bid five clubs over four hearts.

So, on the one hand it is claimed that four clubs shows both minors, on the other the four diamond bidders intend to make it clear later. Is there truly a clear path?

HIRON: 4NT. This can't possibly be Blackwood once I was unable to bid two spades over one spade. Now partner will choose his better minor, bidding six with the right cards.

KOKISH: Double. Only because I have no bid to elicit the minor suit preference that could lead to a cold slam. If partner pulls to four clubs or four diamonds, perhaps we'll survive.

The last phrase was ironical.

This was the marking:

CALL	AWARD	PANEL
4♣	10	5
4◇	10	4
Double	7	3
4NT	6	3
3NT	4	1
Pass	2	0

The Director remarked that no one had chosen four spades. True, that would be no more daft than some of the other selections. Four hearts is a possibility, too.

Let's be realistic about this: what are the chances that partner will have enough to produce a game? He might have six hearts to the king or Q J, but there will still be three losers in a minor-suit contract and probably four losers in hearts.

You are playing IMPs and the way to gain on this hand is to aim at a plus score when the other North–South pair will be conceding anything from 50 to 300. There are just two sensible calls: Pass, probably worth 50, and four diamonds, possibly worth 130. Note that four diamonds is a better choice than four clubs. If partner has similar values in each suit, probably x x x, it will be easier to control the play in diamonds than in clubs. (All good players know this – with equal length play in the suit that lacks 'tops'.)

It may not be far wrong to double, because the odds are that they will go one down; but it's no certainty and the advantage of taking 100 instead of 50 is small.

22

Bridge World
Director: Alfred Sheinwold

Pairs, N–S vul. You, South, hold:

♠ A 6 5
♡ A 7 4
♢ A 9 6 5 4 2
♣ A

South	West	North	East
1◇	2♣	dble	3♣
?			

Two spades, at this score, is a weak jump overcall, and North's double is negative.

Director: Few panelists had any clear idea of what to do, which may account for the fact that a clear majority chose the action (double) that gave partner most options.

North should be able to work out the nature of the South hand: not more than three spades, from the nature of the East–West bidding, hence not more than three cards in either of the unbid suits (since South would prefer to bid a new suit rather than double with only three spades). But South must have at least 16 points in high cards for his penalty double and cannot have 3–3– 4–3 from his failure to open with 1NT. Hence South must have a 16- or 17-point hand with five or six diamonds and no side length.

If North has a diamond fit he should take the double out. With most other hands he should let the double stand. (He has already denied having a clear-cut bid of his own by choosing a negative double rather than a bid.)

If partner has positive diamond support, why doesn't he support diamonds in preference to the negative double? I would be inclined, at this point, to place him with something like:

♠ x ♡ Q J x x ◇ K x x ♣ Q x x x x

Most of the panel favoured a double, though attributing different senses to it. Thus:

KAPLAN: Double. Penalties, but not absolutely so on the auction. Partner will surely take out with a diamond fit, and surely pass if short in diamonds. Either way, I'm happy.

STERN: Double. Cooperative-business. I expect partner to pull with an undisclosed fit. (I will raise four diamonds to six.) Otherwise, I'll take my sure profit, perhaps at the loss of a few IMPs.

Surprisingly, the player most responsible for the development of negative doubles twenty years earlier made no mention of them now.

ROTH: 4♡. Impossible problem. One of the rare cases where I will bid a three-card suit in preference to any other bid. There is no good bid available, so I will take my chances on finding a 4–3 fit. Other choice is to bid four spades and then five diamonds over five clubs.

Support for this action came from:

WOLFF: 4♠. And convert five clubs to five diamonds. I'm partial to aces.

And there were those who seemed confident that they would find diamond support:

FRIEND: 5◇. After the negative double, I believe I should bid this hand as though diamonds have been supported. Even three small diamonds will be enough if partner has the expected singleton spade.

The Venezuelan champion discovered another virtue in a diamond leap and took a side-swipe at weak jump overcalls.

BERAH: 6$\diamond$. Partner appears to have a singleton spade, and although he has hearts and clubs, he has room left for some diamonds . . . I don't know if it will make, but neither do the opponents. My confident attitude will induce the non-vulnerable adversaries to run for shelter. This is the frequent destiny of weak jump bids.

I don't think it's sound to assume that partner must have diamond support. Players double (do they not?) with such as:

$\spadesuit$ x x $\heartsuit$ Q 10 x x $\diamond$ Q x $\clubsuit$ K J x x x

It is quite possible, at this vulnerability, for the adverse spades to be 6–2.

This was the marking:

CALL	AWARD	PANEL
Dble	100	17
4$\heartsuit$	50	5
4$\diamond$	50	4
4$\spadesuit$	50	4
5$\diamond$	30	2
6$\diamond$	20	1
Abstain	—	1

Why one panelist abstained is not disclosed; did not like the negative double, presumably.

It's a difficult problem, but I think on the whole that double is right. If partner passes, then to take 300 or so may be the best you can do. If partner takes out the double into four diamonds you will probably end in six.

23

IPBM

Director: Joe Amsbury

IMPs, none vul. You, South, hold:

♠ 8 4
♡ A J 9 2
♢ A K
♣ K J 9 8 3

South	West	North	East
1♣	No	1♢	No
1♡	No	1♠	No
?			

This situation is a little awkward because you don't want to make a minimum bid and no brilliant alternative suggests itself. A low-level bid such as two clubs might be passed by a responder who held only 9–10 points. It would be unsound to rebid in notrumps, as you have no guard in spades. Sometimes, in this kind of position, you can *raise* the fourth suit, not suggesting a guard in it, but at this level two spades would suggest spade support. All the panelists were aware of this problem.

ARMSTRONG: 3♣. I'd like to bid two spades to show this type, but I play it as natural. Perhaps three spades might be enlisted, but it sounds natural, too.

Director: Sure. Two spades equals 4–4–1–4 minimum. You have to bid three spades with a good hand and the same shape.

BLAKSET: 3♣. Two spades would be natural, and I don't know

whether North promises one more bid in your methods. I think not, so I have no alternative.

KLINGER: 2♣. Should show the stronger version of the two-club rebid.

I don't see that. With a minimum 2–4–2–5 type it is normal to follow the sequence 1♣–1◇–1♡.

KOKISH: 2♣. A great problem. Can't bid notrumps with no spade stopper, and three clubs feels wrong. Two diamonds suggests a different hand, so we are left with an inadequate two clubs that North should attempt to raise on any excuse.

Two diamonds may not express the hand exactly, but it is more likely than two clubs to keep the ship afloat. So:

REESE: 2◇. Since no fifth suit is available, you must just look for a bid that tells a little more about your values.

STABELL: 2◇. North will bid again, I assume. Observe that two spades indicates spade support.

FLINT: 2◇. Man who bids fourth suit promises one more bid. Confucius he should say.

The usual accurate monthly forecast:

COLLINGS: 3◇. 'Away in a manger' all by myself, but I cannot think of another bid opposite game values. So I have a doubleton spade and a diamond too few.

He means simply that there should be game values in the combined hands. However, players tend to bid the fourth suit when they are simply stumped for a sensible call. Thus on the present occasion North might be no better than:

♠ x x x   ♡ K x x   ◇ Q 9 x x x   ♣ A x

You might think that three diamonds would be a solecism – but far from it!

FORRESTER: 3◇. I play two spades as natural here, so the hand is a bit fixing. Inventing a third diamond is not too bad, so I'll do that for now.

HIRON: 3◇. Good problem! The raise of the fourth suit is
    unacceptable as I might genuinely hold four of them. Three
    diamonds must be the best of a bad lot.
KEHELA: 3◇. Each possibility is worse than the next.
PENCHARZ: 3◇. All right, I am being a slave to point count, but
    I can't bring myself to bid only two diamonds, which would
    be right on:

♠ x x ♡ A J x x ◇ A x ♣ K J x x x

Would it really? I would bid a simple two clubs.

This was the marking:

CALL	AWARD	PANEL
3◇	10	10
3♣	8	4
2◇	7	3
2♣	5	3
1NT	4	1
2♠	4	1
2NT	4	1

The last three answers, evidently, were from panelists who did
not espouse the fourth-suit style.
    The problem raises two questions:
    (1) What is the minimum for fourth suit at the one level?
    (2) As the bidding has gone, which rebids by the opener are
forcing for one round at least, and which are not?
    The effective answer to (1) is that most players would bid one
spade on the moderate hand I quoted above (under Collings's
answer). As for (2), my own idea when I answered two
diamonds was that 1NT and two clubs would be non-forcing. It
is a somewhat uncharted area, where regular partnerships need
to reach an agreement.

24

Bridge International
Director: Bill Pencharz

Pairs, N–S vul. You, South, hold:

♠ A 7 5
♡ 9 7 3
♢ A 6
♣ A K Q 9 8

South	West	North	East
1♣	No	1♡	1♠
?			

Pencharz took on the role of competition editor at short notice in 1985 and repeated a number of problems from 1974. Those who set these problems quite often test the panel with a problem from an earlier year, ostensibly as a means of discovering whether bidding techniques have altered. For people like myself who have no memory, this is a blind trap: perhaps your answer will be in direct opposition to the learned comments you made on a previous occasion. The new editor was the first to fall into the pit.

HIRON (1974): 2NT. 'Calm of mind, all passion spent.' Twenty years ago I would have bid two diamonds and defended my choice to the death. Ten years ago I might have fluttered with two spades. But now, in the twilight of my bidding years, 2NT.

HIRON (1985): 2♢. A nice safe manufactured reverse. Forcing in any sensible system. Perhaps not according to the conditions of this contest, but I'll still bid it.

Director: After twilight comes darkness and, presumably, after darkness, death. Not that I am suggesting that Hiron is yet actually dead. I think it's more that the very young (Hiron in 1954) had a great affinity with the old (Hiron in 1985).

BENJAMIN (1974): 2♠. It may be important for North to become the notrump declarer.

BENJAMIN (1985): 2◇. It may be advantageous, if notrumps is reached, for North to be the declarer.

It's the same thought, almost. Here too:

SHEEHAN (1974): 2♡. A real brute. At least two hearts works out best if there is further bidding. To bid notrumps now might be a mistake if partner has Q x of spades, and to bid two spades now (as I am sure some will) overstates the hand too much.

Sheehan makes the same bid (and is in the same minority of one) in 1985.

HAUSLER: 2♠. Maybe a slight overbid, but it leaves open the road to the most probable games, four hearts and 3NT, played by North.

ROWLANDS: 2♠. I would like to play double as a 2NT rebid without a guard, which allows more room, but with this lot I don't mind the slight overbid of two spades.

These panelists refer to the 'slight overbid'. There's nothing slight about it. Two spades is forcing to game. Yes, we have a good hand, but surely it's not that good?

However, there is good sense in this answer:

SCHROEDER: 2♠. It always pays when the right hand plays the contract – even when you are one level too high.

Four of the panel bid 1NT. These are Victor Mollo (who bid 2NT in 1974 – is age wearying him?) and three of our overseas panelists, Garozzo, Helness, and:

SOLOWAY: 1NT. Showing 15–17 and that I was going to bid 2NT until the interference.

Pencharz agreed with the following:

FORRESTER: 2NT. Hard to believe that you can split the panel on this one.

KELSEY: 2NT. I used to worry about these situations, but now I just make the value bid without straining the brain too much.

KANTAR: 2NT. Seven tricks are seven tricks.

This was the marking in 1974:

CALL	AWARD	PANEL
2♣	10	7
2♦	9	5
2♡	6	1
3♣	5	1
2NT	5	3

Who bid three clubs, did you ask? I did, remarking that the objections to three clubs, apparently a palooka bid, were less serious than to the other choices. By 1985 more panelists (including myself) were ready to accept the value bid of 2NT:

CALL	AWARD	PANEL
2NT	10	8
2♦	6	3
2♠	5	4
1NT	4	4
2♡	1	1

Although the text implied that Sheehan recommended two hearts, in the tabulated list his answer appeared as two spades. Perhaps the printers couldn't bear two hearts.

It's a better hand than '17 points' suggests. I think 1NT is ridiculous, and two diamonds I don't understand at all. I would rather bid three hearts than two hearts.

25

Bridge World
Director: Robert Wolff

IMPs, both vul. You, South, hold:

♠ 3
♡ A K 9 8 7 4 2
♢ 4 2
♣ J 6 4

South	West	North	East
—	No	1♣	No
1♡	dble	No	4♠
?			

Director: Anything could be right here, including five clubs (I hope East has spades and diamonds for his leap to four spades, but he could have spades and clubs), and there are tons of IMPs at stake. I'm usually wrong in bidding on in positions like this, but here I go again – like the majority of the panel, I go for five hearts.

VON EISNER: 5♡. Tough! If they can make four spades, and I'm inclined to think they can, no world-shattering disaster should result [in five hearts]. And if they take the push to five spades, great!

KAHN: 5♡. It is too dangerous to defend four spades.

Others are bidding to make, or having it both ways.

ROBINSON: 5♡. Perhaps partner has

♠ x x x ♡ x ♢ A Q x ♣ K Q x x x

and we will make it. Perhaps he doesn't, and we will be down 1100.

RUBIN: 5♡. This could easily be a two-way game, so believe the enemy. (Note that partner ought not to own a tripleton heart.)

Others draw a rather different inference from North's pass over West's double.

HARDY: 5♡. Partner's pass of the double shows some willingness to play hearts. If five hearts fails, four spades probably makes.

CARAVELL: 5♡. Partner's pass suggests a doubleton heart to me. Still, pass is a close second choice, since East's action suggests he might have clubs.

Yes, I think that's right. Remember that West had passed originally; how, then, could East leap to four spades on a balanced hand? It is much more likely that he has strong clubs and perhaps 5–1–2–5 shape.

For a substantial minority, pass was the first choice.

GERARD: Pass. Insurance could be expensive. Even opposite

♠ K x x ♡ Q x x ◇ K J x ♣ A x x x

we're down two in five hearts, against a likely plus. And partner needn't have hearts or a balanced hand for his pass, but could easily own, say,

♠ K x x ♡ x ◇ A Q x x ♣ K x x x x

I wouldn't be surprised if *double* were the winning call.

And just two panelists made the point that strikes me about this problem:

KAPLAN: Pass. I have an ace-king opposite an opening bid, so I expect to beat them, particularly since partner, over the double, neither raised hearts nor rebid clubs. He has a normal high-card opening and we have no great fit, so it would be an error to let the opponents panic me to the five level. I'd rather double four spades than bid five hearts.

Incidentally, anyone who complains about the failure to *pre-empt*, with this good hand and bad suit, doesn't understand the game.

Just in case it didn't register, that last sentence was bitter irony. Kaplan's opinion was that South should have responded four hearts on the first round.

GRANOVETTER: Pass. Serves us right for not bidding four hearts on the round before! That's the *only point* of this problem.

This was the marking:

CALL	AWARD	PANEL
5♡	100	20
Pass	60	10
Double	20	0
4NT	20	0
5♣	20	0

Double had some support among competitors, though not from the panel. 4NT, extending a choice between five hearts and five clubs, would be sensible with 6–4 in the two suits, but not when they are 7–3.

As a rule, in this book, I have avoided problems where there might be argument about the earlier bidding, but this one has interesting features. *Of course* it is sensible to respond four hearts to one club, thus avoiding the subsequent dilemma. Responses at the one level already cover too wide a range. What to do as the bidding has gone? Well, if the inference is correct that East has spades and clubs, not spades and diamonds, the best action may be to pass and lead a trump. With clubs stacked on the right, I wouldn't expect to make five hearts.

26

IPBM

Director: Joe Amsbury

IMPs, E–W vul. You, South, hold:

♠ 10
♡ K 2
◇ A 5 4
♣ A 9 8 7 6 4 2

South	West	North	East
—	—	1◇	No
2♣	No	2♡	No
?			

Director: Back on the commonsense theme. A reverse after a two-level response is ostensibly game-forcing. Nowadays, even the traditional escape route of responder rebidding his own suit is regarded as forcing – ♠ x x x ♡ K x ◇ K x ♣ A Q J 9 x x, for instance. To be able to bid three clubs, forcing, is more descriptive than waffling through the fourth-suit maze and never attaining clarity of communication.

Very good, Joe! I could not, as they say, have put it better myself. There were, of course, some supporters here for the fourth suit.

PENCHARZ: 2♠. Clearly we are in the slam zone. Clubs could easily play better than diamonds, so let's look for support.

It's not so likely that partner will have positive support for a seven-card suit that has been bid only once. I mean, if you fancy clubs, why not rebid them?

REBATTU: 2♠. I could support diamonds, but partner might still have a club fit. If he bids 2NT I can support diamonds anyway.

SHARPLES: 2♠. It costs nothing to investigate cheaply. We are unlikely to settle for less than the small slam but there may be more in it.

And there were those who preferred to support diamonds rather than rebid clubs:

KOKISH: 3◇. Very tough. Three clubs is fine, too. Were the ♣ 2 the ♣ 10, I'd guess 3♣ instead.

ARMSTRONG: 3◇. We're in a game-forcing situation. I don't think the clubs are strong enough to rebid.

Sorry, I'll give you eight next time.

FORRESTER: 3◇. We'll start there as seven diamonds looks the most likely grand slam. I will not stop out of six diamonds (at least), but it is best to set trumps unambiguously as I wish to bid four hearts *en route*.

PRICE: 3◇. What an enormous hand this has become! I hope that the system allows me to bid three diamonds forcing (personally I would regard three clubs as forcing, too), following which I shall do a lot more bidding. The alternative bid of four diamonds takes up too much space.

WERDELIN: 3◇. If he bids 3NT I will follow with four clubs.

I reckon three clubs gets you to the cold six clubs; anything else to the fair six diamonds.

This was the marking:

CALL	AWARD	PANEL
3◇	10	9
2♣	8	6
3♣	7	2
4◇	5	3
4♣	4	1

It may not matter in the end what you do at this point, but I must say I do not understand the support for two spades. Three clubs leaves almost as much space and conveys important information. Nor can I see why three diamonds is preferred. If North has six diamonds, or a strong five-card suit, he can rebid it over three clubs.

My own vote was for four clubs, because I wasn't sure that three clubs would be regarded as forcing. In that area I see that I was old-fashioned. Responses at the two level, and also reverse bids, are taken more seriously than they used to be.

27

Bridge World
Director: Alfred Sheinwold

IMPs, none vul. You, South, hold:

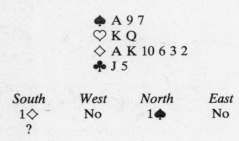

♠ A 9 7
♡ K Q
♢ A K 10 6 3 2
♣ J 5

South	West	North	East
1♢	No	1♠	No
?			

Quite a common, and always an awkward, situation: you have
the values for three spades, or three diamonds, or 2NT, but
each of these bids has disadvantages. There is another
possibility, too. Sheinwold began with this forthright statement:

*Director: When the history of the United States is written a
hundred years from now, much bewilderment will be expressed
over the blindness that afflicted American bridge players during
the autumn of 1971. Nobody will know why 23 panelists voted
for three diamonds in this problem, while only 4 saw the merit of
bidding two hearts.*

Reading on, one finds that he regards the reverse as forcing. I
dare say it is in the Kaplan–Sheinwold system. Still, I wonder
what one is supposed to do as responder with a weak 4–3–2–4
type. I don't mind treating a bid as forcing when both players
are marked with values – as when responder has bid at the two
level – but it has always seemed to me that if minimum bids are

forcing there is no way to stop the gravy train on bad hands. The majority (as you already know) thought that three diamonds was the best answer.

ROTH: 3◇. You should be ashamed to present this problem. There is no correct answer! Perhaps the best opening bid would have been 1NT!

If you can bear to open 1NT I don't see why you shouldn't now rebid 2NT.

KAPLAN: 2♡. Not dangerous, since if North raises hearts viciously he will have five spades. This bid shows my strength while preserving both notrump and spade chances.

RUBENS: 2♡. If partner raises hearts he should have five spades. When I then support spades he will *not* assume I necessarily have a singleton club – just a normal 3–3–5–2 reverse.

HAZEN: 2♣. This may get me a low score or zero, but a fair approach is to penalize the zero bid – two diamonds. Low scores should then go to three spades or three diamonds.

From what follows, it appears that he regarded 3♣ and 3◇ as inferior because they committed the partnership to game.

We may as well dispose of other low-rated bids before seeing what the blind majority had to say.

EHRLENBACH: 3♠. All other bids are square pegs in round holes.

BELL: 2NT. We can make three notrumps if North has J x x of hearts and club values, yet partner may have no safe action if opener's rebid is the second-best call, three diamonds.

Now for a few comments from the majority.

OAKIE: 3◇. Regardless of what bidding system is used, it has always been axiomatic that a jump rebid shows some interest in the response partner has made. With this hand that's the message I want to transmit: 'I have a good hand, plenty of diamonds, and I can stand to hear you rebid your spades.'

And you've shown the J 5 of clubs as well, I suppose.

LAWRENCE: 3◇. The right 'nothing' bid. Would love to be playing any kind of club system on this and similar hands.

RUBIN: 3◇. I prefer this to two hearts, although I don't object to the latter. No bid is really productive.

And none of these answers was very productive, either. This was the marking:

CALL	AWARD	PANEL
3◇	100	23
2♡	70	4
3♠	50	4
2NT	20	1
2♣	20	1

Three diamonds may be a reasonable expression of the values, but it has the substantial disadvantage that if partner bids 3NT your hand, with the two doubletons, will be exposed on the table. I am sure that at rubber bridge most good players would bid 2NT. Is this necessarily wrong in tournament play? I don't think so. Very often, on this type of hand, one makes a game that could have been defeated by a different defence. For one thing, they quite often attack the spade suit in 3NT. Second choice: three spades, not three diamonds, which should show a hand with more shape, fewer tops.

28

Bridge International
Director: David Bird

IMPs, N–S vul. You, South, hold:

> ♠ —
> ♡ 9 8 6 5
> ◇ J 8 6 4 3
> ♣ K 6 4 2

South	West	North	East
—	—	—	No
No	1♠	dble	4♠
No	No	dble	No
?			

Director: What should we do here? Take the small change from four spades, or look for some resting-place at the five level, hoping for greater reward?

More than half the panel voted for 4NT, a take-out manoeuvre. This is what they said:

SOLOWAY: 4NT. Expect to make our contract. Let partner name the suit.

LEBEL: 4NT. A take-out bid. There should be no problem in finding the right suit if we bid 4NT.

At this level one doesn't always find the *best* suit. Anyway, the immediate problem is whether or not you bid on at all.

HAUSLER: 4NT. North's double is in principle for penalties, because 4NT for take-out is available. The double normally will be based on top tricks, which will come in handy at a five-level contract. The vulnerability is the decisive reason why we should bid on.

COHN: 4NT. We should beat four spades, but the little I have is gold, and we may well make eleven tricks in offence. Besides, they are not going to let us play it.

Well, I'm impressed by the confidence of these panelists that the five level will be safe. I can't allow Cohn's last point, though. When the opponents have bumped the bidding in this fashion they will almost invariably let you stew where you land, hoping that you are too high or too low.

Jourdain thought it possible that partner would take 4NT as two-suited in the minors and considered this a recommendation for 4NT. But (a) partner would be wrong to think that, and (b) you might end in five clubs opposite A J x with a much better fit in hearts.

Freddie North seemed to think he and his partner were in the slam zone and pondered between 4NT and five spades.

Also quaint, Mollo booked a one-way ticket to five hearts.

Let's move on, to those who would rather defend four spades than advance to the five level. They still have my support.

HIRON: Pass. Don't forget that partner could have bid 4NT (*all* suits) if he really wanted me to bid. I have got a king and a jack and, as I am sure TR will say, four tricks are easier to make than eleven.

REESE: Pass. Why try to make eleven tricks instead of four, especially as you can't be sure of finding the best contract.

LAVINGS: Pass. There is no point in taking the double out if you are going down in your call.

Oh dear, one of our Australian panelists is going to lapse into verse. Steel yourselves!

MCNEIL: Pass. There are bold players,
And old players,
But few old bold players.

Well, it rhymed a treat, even if it didn't seem to scan very well.

This was the marking:

CALL	AWARD	PANEL
4NT	10	12
Pass	9	10
5♡	1	1

Surely the point made by Alan Hiron is unanswerable: if North had wanted to battle on he would have bid 4NT instead of doubling. Also, the South hand, with its lack of intermediates, is not really a prime candidate for eleven tricks.

29

IPBM

Director: Joe Amsbury

Pairs, none vul. You, South, hold:

♠ J 8 6
♥ K Q
♦ K Q J 9
♣ A K 8 4

South	West	North	East
—	—	—	1♠
dble	No	2♥	2♠
?			

You would have preferred to overcall with 1NT instead of the double? So would I, and so would the Director, but this was the second part of a problem and the majority did not dispute the double on the first round.

Now, what do you do over two spades? A simple solution was advanced by:

PALOOKA: Pass. Secure in the knowledge that there are always some who bid the same as me (*sic*). If this applies – and you print their reasons – I will know why I did it.

Director: Well, you won't get a lot of help from Collings, who passed with no comment, or from Forrester, who passed, adding 'Is this a problem?' There was some comment from the 'action' men:

HIRON: Double. Suggesting more high cards than I have already shown. Partner can decide, but he will appreciate that I'm not charmed by his hearts.

So you are treating the second double as a further take-out double? We used to say that a double when partner had shown a suit was a penalty double. Still, it may well be right that a second double of the *same* suit should be for take-out. This was the view of:

SHEEHAN: Double. I would have passed two hearts, lacking a sensible bid, but I think a double of two spades probably indicates this hand type – after all, I didn't bid 1NT.

He means that with strong spades he would not have doubled on the first round.

ROWLANDS: Double. This should show heart tolerance, both minors and extra values. At least, this isn't too wide of the mark compared with the cost of some of my bids.

That all seems to make sense.

But some panelists took the old-fashioned view that a second double would be a penalty double. At any rate, they were not prepared to put it to the test.

MARX: Pass. East's further bid leaves me well placed to pass.

SHARPLES: Pass. This might produce an indifferent score but seems to have the edge on the alternatives, any of which could end in some kind of disaster.

There are positive disasters and negative disasters. Two spades passed out with ten tricks cold in a minor which for our side is a minor disaster. Two spades, down two, with 3NT cold for us is a positive disaster. Boy, am I glad that I wouldn't be in this 'guess what kind of disaster' situation!

True, you can avert the disaster on this hand by overcalling with 1NT on the first round. But with something like A x in spades and a 19 count you have to double, and then this particular problem – the meaning of a subsequent double of two spades – cannot be avoided.

That the present hand is difficult was attested by:

FLINT: Don't know. This is permitted in all political quizzes – why not here?

Because we reckon to have a panel who do know how they are going to vote. What do you do at the table?

Flint's answer nevertheless expresses the true fact that any action you may take at this point is borderline.

This was the marking:

CALL	AWARD	PANEL
Pass	10	12
Double	7	7

You may hazard a double if you accept the Hiron–Sheehan–Rowlands presumption that the double simply shows extra values, not determination to defeat the contract.

It is true that if you pass you won't get a great score on the board, but it may not be worse than average. There is a further point which, I dare say, Jack Marx had in mind: partners tend to respond two hearts on a moderate 2–4–2–5 type, such as ♠ x x ♡ J 9 x x ◇ A x ♣ 10 x x x x. If you pass over two spades it is possible that partner will be able to come again.

30

Bridge World
Director: Kit Woolsey

Pairs, none vul. You, South, hold:

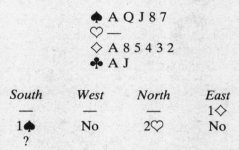

♠ A Q J 8 7
♡ —
◇ A 8 5 4 3 2
♣ A J

South	West	North	East
—	—	—	1◇
1♠	No	2♡	No
?			

Some partnerships might treat the two-heart response as forcing, but that is not the usual practice. The Director established his position early on:

Understandably, nobody was happy with his choice on this hand. Everyone agreed that three diamonds would be a cue-bid, not a natural call, so arriving at a diamond partial is out of the question.

A majority of the panel went conservative. Two spades has the slight advantage of keeping the lines open, but may well get us to the wrong part score, or too high if North's hand is suitable only for play in hearts. Passing speaks for itself – it works or it doesn't.

KANTAR: Pass. And take my zero. I have found that no matter what I do with these hands, I always get a zero.
RUBIN: 2♠. You're dead, so bid like a zombie.

You have taken your own advice there. I would bet any money that there would be more tricks in hearts than in spades.

HAZEN: 2♠. There's no system I know of that accepts three diamonds as a suit. I can't imagine that partner can come close to guessing my distribution, therefore a fearful two spades.

KOYTCHOU: Pass. My hand should be more useful as dummy than his. Partner should have something like:

♠ x   ♡ Q J 10 8 7 x   ◇ x x   ♣ 10 x x x

It is true that two hearts would play better, but who, with this rubbish, makes a free bid in response to partner's simple overcall?

ROBINSON: Pass. With the unlikelihood of a fit. I think that two hearts will do better than two spades. He should be able to ruff either diamonds or spades, making his small trumps.

Yes, that's how I see it. Is not North likely to hold something of this sort:

♠ x x   ♡ K Q 10 9 x x   ◇ x   ♣ Q 10 x x

Now two hearts plays very prettily, because you will go on ruffing in hand. You might even end up with ten tricks.

However, some optimists were willing to take the plunge into uncharted waters.

MILES: 3◇. My hunch is that we belong in four hearts, but it would look strange to jump there without giving partner another chance to show belated support for spades. Partner will probably guess from the opponents' silence plus his own shortness that I have diamond length, but I can't imagine that he would pass three diamonds whatever he has.

KOKISH: 2NT. Extra values deserve one more bid, perhaps leading to minus 300 rather than minus 50 (at two hearts). Maybe North has only mediocre hearts but some key notrump fillers. But pass is so damned appealing, isn't it?

MCCALLUM (Karen): 2NT. What a noxious problem! By the way, at the table I would pass one diamond, planning to jump in spades at my next opportunity. That shows primary diamonds with spades (a sensible, if old-fashioned, treatment, still employed by a handful of players).

I haven't met them.

This was the marking:

CALL	AWARD	PANEL
Pass	100	11
2♠	90	11
3♢	50	4
2NT	40	3

The American tournament players, despite Miles's answer, all seem to think that three diamonds on the second round would be a cue-bid. It could, I suppose, be a way of saying 'I have quite a good hand, with some support for hearts.' Still, there is a good case for playing it as natural in this type of sequence. I don't suggest that it would be right here, because I would expect partner to make a lot of tricks in hearts. The panelists who were afraid of playing in hearts were – to put it in my usual charitable way – dozing.

PART IV
WHAT'S GOING ON?

31

Bridge World
Director: Alan Truscott

IMPs, none vul. You, South, hold:

♠ 4
♡ K 3
♢ Q 10 6 2
♣ A K J 9 5 3

South	West	North	East
—	1♠	No	2♡
3♣	3♡	4♢	4♡
?			

That four-diamond bid by a player who passed over one spade –
is it possible? Just about, if you think he would have passed on
such as:

♠ Q x x   ♡ x   ♢ K J 9 x x x   ♣ Q x

  The majority of the panel accepted it as natural, but the
Director gave them little space.

COHN: 5♢. Why should they go one down when we can? If I'm
    wrong it's an easy and uncostly way to look like an
    idiot . . .

One supporter of five diamonds was more perceptive:

SOLOMON: 5♢. This seems too logical. I have a feeling that
    partner holds five cards in clubs and the four-diamond bid
    is lead-directing, in which case 4NT is the best bet. With
    my favourite partners this would be my choice. In a panel
    survey, five diamonds is more on the track.

Director: In future, Mr S, please make what you think is the right bid. You are not expected to guess the lowest common denominator of the hoi polloi.

Whether partner's diamonds are a real suit or not, it can hardly be wrong to give partner space in which to declare himself.

PENDER: 4NT. Partner's four-diamond call seems incongruous in light of his previous pass, therefore strongly suggesting a lead along with a save in clubs. As I am willing to save, I go along but leave room for partner to clarify his intentions.

KANTAR: 4NT. I think this is my partner's way of sacrificing at five clubs if I don't think a diamond lead can defeat four hearts. Just in case he has long diamonds I give him a choice. He should have:

♠ 10 x x x x x   ♥ x x   ♦ A   ♣ Q 10 x x

Covering a different possibility:

RUBENS: 4NT. Since partner has diamond values, I must bid on; but I cannot commit the hand to diamonds, for North might hold such as:

♠ x x x   ♥ x x x   ♦ A K x   ♣ Q x x x

A different bid, but same general idea, came from:

KAPLAN: 4♠. Partner's four-diamond bid is so odd, considering that he passed over one spade, that I must allow for some devious lead-directing master bid. For this purpose four spades is better than 4NT: if partner was kidding with diamonds he bids five clubs; if he *has* diamonds and wants to know what I am up to, *he* can bid 4NT.

Confident that partner was intending to support clubs:

SHEINWOLD: 5♣. (Second choice: four spades.) North must have club support since otherwise his bid of four diamonds out of the blue would make no sense (in view of his previous pass).

There were two far-fetched minority choices:

99

GOLD: Double. Four diamonds in this sequence should be lead-directing. If partner is operating he'll pull.

ROTH: Pass. The bidding is impossible. Why did partner now bid four diamonds when he could not overcall on the first round with two diamonds or three diamonds? He must have spades, and he might even be cute with a club fit. Pass and see what he does.

The veteran expert turns a few circles here. The bidding is impossible; he must have spades; he might have a club fit.

This was the marking:

CALL	AWARD	PANEL
5♢	100	24
4♠	90	1
4NT	90	10
5♣	70	2
Pass	30	1
Dble	20	1

I blush for the panel on this one.

Well, yes, it is true that five diamonds might catch partner on the wrong foot – though I'd be inclined to say that it was his fault if he was not prepared for a raise. No doubt, 4NT covers more possibilities. If partner has the diamond hand I envisaged above, he can bid five diamonds; if not, five clubs.

32

Bridge World
Director: Howard Schenken

IMPs, E–W vul. You, South, hold:

> ♠ A 8 5 3
> ♡ 7 3 2
> ◇ 9 7 2
> ♣ A 5 3

South	West	North	East
—	1♠	2♡	2♠
3♡	4♣	5♣	No
?			

There are only two possible answers to this problem, but the Director raises some very interesting points. He begins by quoting from the minority who proposed reverting to five hearts.

JACOBY: 5♡. Code XYZ – a code I suggest be adopted as Bridge World Standard for the perennial 'What's the problem?'

Director: A problem with only two reasonable answers gives the Director very little difficulty with the marking. Scorer, give that man 60 points.

ROBINSON: 5♡. I play five clubs as a slam try, but the spade ace may be opposite a void.

SCRIVENS: 5♡. One might be tempted to bid six hearts, but the weak trump holding and absence of a diamond honour should dampen our enthusiasm.

KANTAR: 5♡. What else with a wasted ace?

At about this time an attempt was made to codify a system by reference to Bridge World Standard. Schenken thought there should be an addition to the list. He commented:

I have been a bit sceptical about the potential merits of Bridge World Standard, but the results of this problem have made me look upon it with rather more favour. It would be comprehensible if it had been one panelist; perhaps even if it had been two panelists. But when three (perhaps more) interpret a bid as a slam try when the majority regard it as an attempted sacrifice, something is, to be very restrained about it, wrong.

I can see only one excuse for a bid of five hearts and one panelist offered it:

ROTH: 5♡. Playing safe. Partner may be being fancy.

After accepting this possibility, the Director observed that the five-club bid could not have been intended to direct a lead, since North himself would be on lead against an opposing spade contract. Look at it how you will, the only explanation for the five-club bid is that North would be happy to play in clubs. The majority agreed.

WEISS: Pass. I see no point to North's five-club bid unless it is to suggest a suit that may be longer than the heart suit.

FREIER: Pass. I can't see North bidding five clubs unless his clubs are as long as or longer than his hearts.

RUBIN: Pass. Partner may own six clubs and five hearts.

Some pass either because (1) they haven't yet been doubled, or (2) they hope partner will read the pass to five clubs as lead-directional should opponents continue to five spades. Jubilant in this interpretation:

WALSH: Pass. A lead-directing pass against the potential five spades doubled – what a novel situation.

Taking the best of both possible worlds:

102

WOLFF: Pass. Partner may have five hearts and six clubs. Also, I want to indicate a club lead against five spades.

To which Howard responded with both sense and style:

I regret I must say that the dual interpretation is a bit inconsistent. If the auction indicates that partner probably has more clubs than spades, South must pass five clubs on many hands with which he does not want a club lead, simply to ensure that his side will play the correct suit at the five level. In fact, in view of the vulnerability and South's two aces, it seems unlikely that the opponents will venture any further. The lead-directional pass idea, however well founded it may be in theory, seems to be an excuse for passing rather than a reason.

This was the marking:

CALL	AWARD	PANEL
Pass	100	25
5♡	60	8

All the evidence is that partner is 5–6 in hearts and clubs. If the opponents lead spades, five hearts may be playable even if the suit breaks 4–1, but it is quite likely that the lead will be a diamond, setting up an immediate force. The award of 60 for five hearts was generous.

IPBM

Director: Joe Amsbury

IMPs, N–S vul. You, South, hold:

♠ 8 5 3
♡ K Q J
♢ —
♣ A Q 10 9 8 7 2

South	West	North	East
—	1♢	No	1♠
3♣	3♡	4♣	No
?			

This was the second part of a two-part question, the first part asking panelists whether they agreed with the jump to three clubs. Reaching great heights, the panel supported three clubs by a margin of 19 to 2.

Having overcome that hurdle, what are you going to do over partner's unexpected four spades? The first answer reflects the bewilderment that many players might feel.

PALOOKA: 5♣. *Four* spades? What does that mean? Can't be to play! He would have bid one spade, at least, over one diamond. Advance cue-bid? Looking for seven? Perhaps not. He is thinking about another hand? He thinks I bid spades? I'll just repeat my suit – when in doubt, and all that.

The Director, clearing the air, as he put it, stated that of course four spades was a cue-bid agreeing clubs.

COLLINGS: 5♢. Automatic. With no losers in spades, opposite a partner who has a lot of diamonds and, who knows, maybe the ace of hearts as well. Six clubs should be a piece of cake.

PRICE: 5◇. With presumably no spade losers opposite I am happy to bid the small slam and hopefully might now hear five hearts.

FORRESTER: 5◇. Four spades is a cue-bid agreeing clubs in my mind, so a slam is very reasonable. However, they may be bidding six spades in a minute and a diamond lead would help our cause no end. Hence the bid.

Director: I think they win the debate. Forrester's comment on the lead situation is important (even though he forgot he would be on lead). If they do bid lots of spades, partner will surely know what to do if he gets in. Meanwhile, North can have the heart ace.

They don't win the debate with me. North passed over one diamond: is he now seriously inviting me to bid six clubs? And where are all the spades? West did not support them. One quite possible explanation of the bidding so far is that North has spade *losers* and is making a rather ordinary attempt to intimidate the opposition and obtain the contract in five clubs.

There were supporters for five clubs:

BROCK: 5♣. Where are the spades – coming from West? Their sacrifice looks very cheap, so I go slowly in an attempt to buy the contract.

Why should West bid three hearts if he has strong support for spades?

FLINT: 5♣. Intending to be pushed.

FORQUET: 5♣. Yes, it seems that North is void in spades. So we are cold for six, but probably we could eventually bid seven.

KEHELA: 5♣. If four spades was a splinter, then our prime objective must be to play the hand. (Splinter signifying a singleton or void in spades.)

LAWRENCE: 5♣. On the assumption that four spades is a control (not necessarily a singleton or void) I bid five clubs. My three small spades are a serious concern.

The jump to four spades, if serious, does not suggest A x x.

The perceptive will note that the votes have appeared in alphabetical order. Perhaps the further down the alphabet, the poorer the judgement.

There were several supporters for six clubs, all for dubious reasons, such as:

REBATTU: 6♣. As partner passed one diamond he has not a strong spade suit, but a void with club support. He must have a lot of diamonds, too, I suppose. The ace of hearts is our only loser.

SOLOWAY: 6♣. If partner is trying to go somewhere I'll go. He should have a spade control and a raise to five clubs.

This was the marking:

CALL	AWARD	PANEL
6♣	10	8
5◇	8	5
5♣	7	7
4NT	6	1

Suppose Collings had been playing with – Collings: how would he have read that four-spade bid? It *might* be a serious well-founded slam try (as he presumed above), but it might also be a loud noise, designed to frighten the opposition and win the contract at an economic level. Mind you, six clubs may be the best tactical manoeuvre: let the opposition do the guessing.

Amsbury attributed this hand to North: ♠ A ♡ 10 9 8 x ◇ Q 10 x x ♣ K J x x. It's more likely that partner (if genuine) has a void in spades. In any case, I would bid 4NT over four spades, intending to pass five clubs.

Bridge World
Director: Alan Truscott

Pairs, none vul. You, South, hold:

♠ A 10 5 4 2
♡ 7 6
♢ A 3
♣ A 8 5 2

South	West	North	East
1♠	2♡	No	3♢
No	No	3♠	No
?			

Director: Almost all the panel laughed heartily at the thought that there could be any alternative action (to a pass). *However, North's bidding does raise a question.*

HUDECEK: Pass. North couldn't act over the two-heart overcall – and *now* he raises the spades! I will have a few questions for him at the end of the hand, questions related to his I.Q., ancestry, and whether he should be permitted to walk the streets.

Assessing the situation more accurately:

WOLFF: Pass. I guess partner has five or six hearts along with his three spades, but so what?

KANTAR: Partner must have five hearts and four spades. Otherwise he has gone berserk.

Not *four* spades, surely? With that holding it would be normal to raise the spades on the first round.

HALPERIN: Pass. I know partner must have a penalty double of two hearts with a fair hand, but he could have bid game himself. He should have:

♠ J x x ♡ K Q 10 x x ♢ x x ♣ K x x x.

An extra card or two always helps.

In case you are still wondering what the problem is about, this answer will give you the idea:

RUBIN: Pass. I would like to return to two spades. Please don't tell me that partner owns a doubleton spade honour and five or six clubs – I cannot stand those auctions.

A few panelists were on that track:

RUBENS: 4♣. Since he did not raise immediately, partner must have an alternative in mind; my spades are horrible.

GOLD: 4♣. Not having given an original free raise, North should have something like:

♠ K x ♡ x x x x ♢ x ♣ K x x x x x

or 2–4–2–5.

KAPLAN: 4♣. My partner would raise directly with three-card support and a smattering of high cards. So I must play North to hold a doubleton spade and long clubs – conceivably five or six of them.

It doesn't follow, surely, that he has long clubs. This was a good answer:

MILES: Pass. What could partner have for this sequence? Perhaps only two spades and four or five clubs:

♠ K x ♡ K x x ♢ x x x ♣ Q J x x x

In this case we belong in clubs. But perhaps he has three spades and passed two hearts because he had good hearts:

♠ J x x ♡ K J 10 8 x ♢ x x ♣ K x x

I am not sure enough of anything to take action.

One panelist, voicing the majority, indulged in the rash pastime of throwing a stone at the director.

COHN: Pass. He couldn't bid two spades over two hearts, and this is supposed to be a problem? Only Truscott (and possibly Miles) will dream up a reason for bidding.

He wasn't quite right, as you have seen. This was the marking:

CALL	AWARD	PANEL
Pass	100	36
4♣	50	3

Four clubs doesn't really stand up, as Miles's second example showed. Still, it was an interesting idea, and less familiar than Rubin's answer suggested. How often have you deliberately raised the level of the contract into a new suit on the grounds that partner must hold better support for the suit that has not been mentioned? There is scope there for an instructive essay.

35

Bridge World
Director: Howard Schenken

IMPs, N–S vul. You, South, hold:

♠ J 6 3
♥ Q J 2
♦ A 9 8 7 4
♣ 7 6

South	West	North	East
—	1♣	dble	1♠
2♦	2♣	dble	3♣
?			

It is a familiar sort of sequence and most tournament players will conclude at once that East has made an old-fashioned type of psychic bid: he has club support and his spade bid was a bluff. The Director wastes no words to explain this.

Director: East's psychic does not make South's hand better nor his spades longer, but still it is surely right for South to bid three spades. This analysis was the most complete:

RUBENS: 3♠. Partner should have five spades and/or extra values, so either way I'm okay. Since I obviously have values, not just diamonds, I have denied holding four spades by not doubling one spade.

Disputing this analysis was:

KANTAR: Pass. I will bid three spades if partner bids three diamonds. If I bid three spades now, partner may think I have four spades.

For goodness' sake, Eddie, wake up! If anything, the opposite conclusion is more likely – that South does *not* hold four spades. As a rule, one has a duty to expose the ancient psychic bid immediately. And why suppose that partner, perhaps with 5–4–2–2 distribution, will be able to bid again? More on the ball:

MILES: 3♠. I'm unlikely to have four spades since I didn't double on the previous round, so I have as good a spade holding as partner can hope. I need to bid spades to prevent the opponents from stealing us blind.

FREY: 3♠. I would like to have four spades, but I think I must bid as if partner had bid the spade suit at the point when he doubled two spades.

The opposite view:

IJAMS: Pass. I will wait and see what my partner does over three clubs.

Other passers said similarly. To summarize, there are two flaws in passing: partner may pass also, and West may bid higher (thus obstructing North).

Assuming you are going to bid, there is some question as to how much.

WOOLSEY: 3♠. Four spades is too aggressive. Partner can see the vulnerability and will bid game with anything extra.

There you are on a slippery slope. Partner may think that you too can see the vulnerability and can make your own decisions in the light of it.

FREIER: 4♠. On the bidding it looks like a perfect hand to jump to four spades and take the pressure off partner.

PAVLICEK: 3♠. Four spades might be even better, but I doubt whether partner will pass three spades with any hand on which ten tricks can be made. Also, I can't disregard the possibility that West has four strong spades for his raise, which could be a nuisance in the play.

111

One panelist gave Schenken the chance for a witty conclusion.

BEGIN: 3♣. Nobody has done this [meaning the ancient psychic of one spade] to me in 35 years, unless it's some little old lady who oozes honesty out of every pore. Maybe, as this practice went out with the bustles, somebody will revive it and get away with it one day.

Yes, the Insufficient Bid Coup has been disallowed in this column for too long. Bring back the old stratagems, I say, before modern science ruins the game.

This was the marking:

CALL	AWARD	PANEL
3♠	100	19
Pass	60	12
4♠	60	2
3♦	20	0
4♣	10	1
3♣	—	1

I dare say that some of the passers were flattered by the award of 60 points. There is no certainty that they even detected East's baby psyche.

Once you have decided that East was bluffing and that North doubled two spades to show a strong holding, surely five cards, do you think that *three* spades is enough on the South hand? It seems to me that South's Q J x of hearts is an important holding and that his hand is well worth four spades, as suggested above by Freier.

36

Bridge International
Director: Albert Dormer

Pairs, N–S vul. You, South, hold:

♠ A Q 6 2
♡ A Q 7 3
♢ 8 4
♣ K J 7

South	West	North	East
—	1♣	2♡	2♠
3♠	4♢	No	4♠
?			

This would be easy enough at rubber bridge or at IMPs: you would take the certain 500 or so from four spades doubled and not be greatly concerned if you found that you could have made 650 your way. At pairs, of course, the situation is different: if you reckon that five hearts is on for you, as you well might in this instance, you must bid it, because you are unlikely to take 700 from four spades doubled.

Director: In judgement situations such as this, the Moderator does best to stand clear, allowing the reader to absorb the panel's accumulated wisdom. These were two opposing views:

REESE: 5♡. In a pairs it is right to play for either 700 or 650 your way. To take 500 may be average or worse.

CROWHURST: Double. If we think the opponents can make four spades, we should not bid five hearts as a sacrifice, since the Law of Total Tricks indicates that this will cost 500.

That is not the sort of argument that I would care to rely on. This Law of Total Tricks business may be sound for most of the time, but surely it has little relevance when there are voids and long suits about. Crowhurst went on:

> The question therefore is whether to bid five hearts because we think we can make it. I think not, for three reasons: the spade holding will be useless offensively, opposite partner's void; after West's bid of four diamonds we shall receive the worst possible lead; and North's pass over four diamonds suggests that he is minimum for his overcall.

The last remark is unsound, surely; North might have various reasons for his pass in this forcing sequence.

These were some further arguments on both sides:

SOLOWAY: 5♡. I seem to have the right values for this contract, but would double at IMPs.

KELSEY: Double. I'm prepared to bet they can't make four spades on a heart lead.

This would be a sound Scottish investment.

JOURDAIN: 5♡. We have no major-suit loser and partner must have outside values in the minors.

LODGE: Double. Five hearts is by no means certain, but beating four spades is if partner leaves it in. Why make a decision if partner can make a better informed one?

Aha! So what's wrong with this?

PRIDAY (Jane): Pass. 110 per cent forcing after the three-spade bid. Actually, it's not easy to construct the layout of this deal, and I've a sneaking feeling that North has made a semi-psyche.

According to the voting, the issue from South's angle is nicely balanced. If partner has any nous at all – which, of course, remains to be proven – it will surely be best to allow him to make the final decision.

114

This was the marking:

CALL	AWARD	PANEL
5♡	10	13
Double	9	13
Pass	1	1

Having recognized the indisputable merit of Jane Priday's answer, I think it was unchivalrous of the Director not to give it a more handsome award.

PART V
SEARCHING FOR TOPS

37

IPBM

Director: Joe Amsbury

Pairs, both vul. You, South, hold:

♠ K 6 4
♡ 9
♢ A 10 6 3
♣ A 10 8 4 3

South	West	North	East
—	1♡	No	2♡
No	No	2♠	No
No	3♡	No	No
?			

A good testing question this, where a very fair argument can be advanced for several alternatives. First, the majority.

ARMSTRONG: 3♠. A close decision, but I think we're likely to make three spades despite partner having a poor suit.

FLINT: 3♠. Has North got a fair hand with poor spades or fair spades in a poor hand? From my strength I deduce the latter.

KELSEY: 3♠. I imagine both sides can make nine tricks, whatever Verne may say.

Although I wrote learnedly about it at the time, I cannot remember exactly what Verne – not Jules, another – did say. The general idea was that if you took note of how many trumps each side was likely to hold in its own contract, this would give you a clue to the total number of tricks each side was likely to make.

ROWLANDS: 3♠. I dislike hanging partner for trying, but I must do something. With some partners I would double, expecting them to have only a four-card suit.

SHARPLES: 3♠. With no show of conviction, as partner is doubtless bidding our cards to some extent and a pass could easily be right. With both partners (North and South) having passed once, how would 2NT over two spades be read? Ideal if we could show spade support and willingness to contest in either minor.

It's too late now, anyway.

PALOOKA: 3♠. But only at pairs. At teams I would bid four! *And* think about redoubling.

Director: Rowlands once remarked, 'When I want protection I'll call the Mafia.' But in today's game of thrust and counter-thrust we do need partner to bail us out when we are in the middle of a crossfire and the evidence is that we are not outgunned.

Quite so; the British style in a pairs event is not to give in readily when opponents have a fit but not enough material for game. The three who voted for pass (the two below and Rebattu) were all overseas contributors.

KLINGER: Pass. Thou shalt not punish thy protector.

KOKISH: Pass. Surely you jest. Should I bury him for his enterprise? I'd sooner double than bid three spades, but neither action has any appeal. You need a fourth spade to begin to think about bidding.

Collings proposed 4♡, which really goes too far, and Sandra Landy 3NT, which is neat in its way. Her argument was that partner was likely to hold only four spades and would therefore have good support for one of the minors.

Then there were the doublers:

PRICE: Double. I don't want to crucify partner, but he is aware that I didn't bid over two hearts and that I have heart shortage. He may have useful hearts and plus 200 would be magic.

SOLOWAY: Double. Partner has hearts. East could not compete to three hearts. Very good defensive hand.

Yes, he makes a good point there. Partner *is* marked with some length in hearts.

REESE: Double. I've a feeling they will go one down. Since South passed two spades, North is free to bid three spades if unsuitable for defence.

This was the marking:

CALL	AWARD	PANEL
3♠	10	9
Double	8	5
Pass	6	3
4♡	4	1
3NT	4	1

Pass seems to me a bit feeble; you won't win any medals if you are going to lose 140, which will surely be their 'optimum', so you may as well try for plus 200. 3NT deserves a better score. Amsbury considers the double 'competitive'; if you accept that description, it is probably right.

Bridge Magazine
Director: Eric Milnes

Pairs, both vul. You, South, hold:

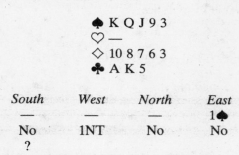

♠ K Q J 9 3
♡ —
♢ 10 8 7 6 3
♣ A K 5

South	West	North	East
—	—	—	1♠
No	1NT	No	No
?			

There are four possible calls, and this is how the Director saw the problem:

Director: Although the double wins the coconut, there is much to be said for all four courses of action; contrariwise there is almost as much to be said against all four. For instance, a double might have the effect of inducing North with a 1–6–3–3 shape to take refuge in two hearts, with which East might be able to deal, or again he might not. You don't want a diamond lead if they buy the contract in two hearts. If you pass you are very likely to get a heart lead; if you bid two spades you are, pace Sheehan and Reese, unlikely to make eight tricks.

There was support for all these choices:

AUHAGEN: Double. A risk worth running in pairs. I want a spade lead instead of a small heart into the jaws of their tenaces.

Worse, a heart honour.

JOURDAIN: Double. Demanding a spade lead and expecting to collect a useful penalty. Players who think this double is for take-out have not analysed the most profitable use of the call; someone who has been unable to contest the opening spade bid will not be encouraged to come into the auction by a 1NT response which may conceal a substantial holding in one of the other suits.

His point, I think, is that partner at any rate will not be inclined to remove the double.

MARX: Pass. The first impulse is to double, if only to ensure a spade lead. But second thoughts introduce a note of caution – a spade lead may not be forthcoming – North may not even have one, and a likely result will be a disastrous heart lead. North can have only 6 or 7 points at most and possibly a good deal less, so he may make the unwelcome move of rescuing into hearts himself.

By *passing* you won't avert a heart lead, will you?

COHN: 2◇. Double is ludicrous – where is the partner so disciplined that he will lead his singleton spade instead of his K Q 10 x x in hearts?

Sitting opposite, I hope.

LE DENTU: 2◇. I would like to beat 1NT, but North is going to lead a heart. Over two diamonds West will bid two hearts, doubled by North for one down!

SHEEHAN: 2♠. Despite the fact that one-spade openings are usually a five-card suit, I consider my chances reasonable of making eight tricks in spades.

Yes, I don't think Milnes was right in implying that it might be difficult to arrive at eight tricks. You may find partner with a trick in diamonds, and in any case you can fight for control by plugging away at this suit. Partner will surely have some protection in hearts.

This was the marking:

CALL	AWARD	PANEL
Dble	10	6
2♢	6	4
Pass	5	2
2♠	5	2

I certainly wouldn't pass and wait feebly for partner to lead a heart from his long suit. If I double or bid two diamonds, the odds are that someone will play in hearts and go one down; I wouldn't be as happy as Le Dentu about defending against two hearts doubled. Two spades our way is likely to produce 110, which will probably be a good score; and if either opponent bids over this he will catch a cold.

39

Bridge World
Director: Alfred Sheinwold

Pairs, N–S vul. You, South, hold:

♠ K 7 4 2
♡ Q J 8 7 3
♢ A 6 4
♣ 2

South	West	North	East
—	—	—	5♢
No	No	dble	No
?			

This is not a common type of problem, if only because opening bids at the five level are rare, but I include it because it gives rise to some interesting reflections.

Director: The important question was whether or not to aim at a slam. The method, though some of the panel did not agree with this sentiment, was secondary.

In the textbooks a double of an opening bid of five is for penalties rather than for take-out; and this meaning would surely be respected at rubber bridge. At match-points, however (i.e. in pairs), South must worry about getting enough to make up for the vulnerable game – or slam – that can be made his way.

The Director went on to make these points: (1) that it would be better to play a slam from his side of the table; (2) that by bidding a slam you may be punishing partner for making a skimpy, but reasonable, move against five diamonds; and (3) that if you bid five hearts you will be showing fair values – not a long suit in a weak hand.

By far the largest vote of the panel, however, was for six diamonds, as expressed in the following answers.

ERDOS: 6$\diamondsuit$. Easiest problem of the set. Any other call, zero.

HUDECEK: 6$\diamondsuit$. My diamond length suggests partner has a void or singleton. The six-diamond bid places the contract badly, however, since West may ruff my diamond ace, or East can lead his singleton.

Having reached this conclusion, he might surely have looked for a different answer.

SCHENKEN: 6$\diamondsuit$. My diamond holding indicates a tremendous fit in one of the majors.

WOLFF: 6$\diamondsuit$. My diamond holding tells me what to do.

Some big guns, you notice, on the side of six diamonds. But note the next answer.

TRUSCOTT: 5NT. At this level we have to guess, and some guess better than others. I am aware that I may be hanging partner if he has taken a chance with his double, but equally we may be lay-down for 12 or 13 tricks.

If I reject the cautious five-heart bid, 5NT must be better than six diamonds for two reasons: better chance to find the 5–4 rather than a 4–4 or 5–3 fit, and better chance to play the contract from my side.

And there was distinguished support for Sheinwold's five hearts.

GAROZZO: 5$\heartsuit$. One of the majors is dividing badly on the auction.

KAPLAN: 5$\heartsuit$. This sounds like a nothing bid, particularly since I am bidding because we may have a slam. But I would not take the double out except for my firm opinion that we can surely make something at the five level and maybe at the six level. So any take-out suggests slam.

MILES: 5$\heartsuit$. I don't want to punish partner for not passing.

I think he may indeed be punishing partner for not passing!
Of the three votes for pass:

ROTH: Pass. A double in balancing position does not guarantee a huge hand. I take my sure profit.

This was the marking:

CALL	AWARD	PANEL
6◇	100	19
6♡	80	8
5NT	80	1
5♡	50	8
Pass	30	3

My feeling about this deal is that the majority of the panel – those who so cheerfully vote for six diamonds – take partner's double altogether too seriously. After all, if an opening five diamonds comes round to you at this vulnerability, and you hold something like A K x x x of clubs and one of the major-suit aces, don't you double, taking the view that if they can make exactly five diamonds you will be getting a poor result anyway?

Second, East has opened five diamonds, missing the ace of trumps, so is likely to hold eight or nine of them, and his distribution may well be 8–4–1–0, or something equally unbalanced. In other words, it may not be good enough for your side to find a 4–4 or 5–3 fit: the suit is likely to break 4–1 or even 5–0.

To pick five hearts out of the air might or might not turn out well. Truscott's 5NT is well reasoned and obviously better than six diamonds. And I think there is much good sense in Roth's brief observation. There probably *is* a better-scoring contract for your side than 300 or so from five diamonds doubled, but can you be sure you will reach it?

126

40

IPBM

Director: Joe Amsbury

Pairs, both vul. You, South, hold:

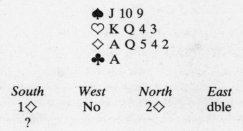

♠ J 10 9
♡ K Q 4 3
♢ A Q 5 4 2
♣ A

South	West	North	East
1♢	No	2♢	dble
?			

Director: It looked a good hand when we picked it up. The immediate support has improved the shining hour, but it is not easy to find out just how high we can go. There is also to be considered the possibility of obtaining a large penalty if the enemy have put their heads on a chopping block.

They have not so far put their heads on any block, as far as I can see. You cannot launch a ferocious attack against two spades, that is certain, and you could not be sure of defeating either two hearts or three clubs. Several panelists were more concerned with reaching a good contract their way.

MARX: 2♡. There is no merit in a policy of masterly inactivity on a hand like this, which may have a bright future. More time is needed to determine where its destiny lies. The most sensible course is to allow the auction to develop as when East had not interfered.

Rob Sheehan, in agreeing with this, made the point that

a redouble would bar you from showing hearts at the two level.

If North is going to raise the diamonds and then bid three clubs, I don't see how you gain by bidding your hearts. But another reason was given in support of the heart bid:

ROWLANDS: 2♡. No reason not to make the natural bid. Perhaps I am biased since six diamonds was the way to a complete top in the E.B.U. Summer Congress and our partnership was the only one to get there. North held: ♠ A ♡ J 10 x ◇ J 10 x x x ♣ 10 9 x x.

You are biased. This was a superlative fit, and North has enough to bid again over an opposing two spades or three clubs.

Now we will have a good idea how the various auctions would have turned out. Without this hindsight, the case for redouble, with its overtones of aggression, seems more likely to carry off the match-points than any pussy-footing call. But let them speak:

COLLINGS: Redouble. I have to get the strength across to my partner. The double has helped and I have four defensive tricks. I will double two hearts, bid three diamonds over two spades, and double three spades if they go on. I'll pass any double by North.

FLINT: Redouble. North might otherwise be nervous of doubling three clubs.

KELSEY: 3◇. The high-card strength may seem to call for a redouble, but I don't want to make it easy for West to come in.

Why on earth not? They could be walking into the jaws of death and your way is allowing a weak West hand to get off the hook. The other votes for three diamonds imply nasty thoughts.

Before relating the nasty thoughts, may I ask what is the best way to lead West into the jaws of death? If you pass and let him bid two spades over the redouble, you won't be able to wield the axe.

WOLFF: 3◇. I'm going to bid it eventually. My opponents are more likely to misjudge their potential under pressure.

REESE: 3◇. You are not going anywhere, but you may promote an indiscretion.

All in all, it appears that you try to make your own best contract by making the natural bid, or you aim for blood by redoubling. In this case you must risk that this may tangle your own communications, if they wriggle clear. For my money, get to your own best contract, it can never lead to disaster.

This was the marking:

CALL	AWARD	PANEL
2♡	10	11
Redble	6	5
3◇	4	2
Pass	1	0

As I see it, two hearts will get you nowhere and redouble will simply warn them to be careful. If they bid over three diamonds you can double, and if partner is very unsuitable he can remove, knowing that you have genuine values in diamonds. Bobby Wolff's answer expresses the situation perfectly. You remember what he said? 'Opponents are more likely to misjudge their potential under pressure.'

41

IPBM

Directors: Joe Amsbury and Brian Senior

Pairs, none vul. You, South, hold:

♠ A K 2
♡ Q 10 5
◇ K Q 6 5 4 2
♣ K

South	West	North	East
1◇	No	1♡	No
?			

Brian Senior, it appears, devised the problems, and Joe
Amsbury commented on the answers. Like a games master who
likes to take his turn at the crease, Amsbury began.

*To me no problem. 1♠. Glad to see a hand when a bid of a
three-card suit is so right and not an operation. All further
bidding (even spade support) is going to be smooth.*

I had a pleasing amount of company.

BROCK: 1♠. For the moment a 14 count and the most flexible
bid is 1♠ – at least if we have to play in four spades it will
be no worse than four hearts, with the forces taken in the
short hand. [Not entirely true, because it may be incon-
venient to ruff with high trumps.] Partner often has four
hearts and five clubs in these positions and hence one spade
may work well. [He means, in the direction of notrumps.]
Both heart raises and diamond rebids, whether to two or
three, are too unilateral – overstating length/strength of
suits respectively.

COLLINGS: 1♠. Not everyone's cup of tea, but let's hear what partner has to say, if anything.

FORRESTER: 1♠. With hearts coming later. It is not often that I bid a non-suit, but two hearts, three hearts, two diamonds, three diamonds, are all so obviously flawed that I have no choice. If I hear two spades I shall begin to regret my decision.

Yes, I made the same point in my answer, but Amsbury replied to Forrester:

Coward! You know at heart that if it goes 2♠–3♡–4♠ you'd happily wait for the dummy to appear.

Others gave much the same answer:

SHARPLES: 1♠. South has an awkward rebid, for the hand is really too good for an immediate two hearts, which doesn't reflect the nature of the hand any more than three diamonds does. So perhaps one spade as a low-level compromise is best.

SOLOWAY: 1♠. No other bid does justice to this hand. Not good enough suit for three diamonds, short of hearts for three hearts. Second choice, two diamonds.

Sheehan actually voted for two diamonds, which strikes me as the most un-British action since – oh well, let's stay away from politics.

ROWLANDS: 1♠, reluctantly. Second choice – three diamonds, third choice – 2NT.

I rather like 2NT, which was formally supported by:

ARMSTRONG: 2NT. Although this is unlikely to be our best part- score, it leaves the game options open.

WOLFF: 3◇. What I don't have here I have there.

Neat comment, if not quite a world champion's analysis.

KELSEY: 3♡. Not ideal, but what is? Three diamonds is a misrepresentation, two hearts is a gross underbid, and one spade is just horrible.

131

PALOOKA: 2♡. An underbid, but not by much if the club king is wasted. Partner's still there, and nothing stimulates more than suit support.

That's true, but while the king of clubs might be wasted, it might also be a most valuable card.

This was the marking:

CALL	AWARD	PANEL
1♠	10	13
3♢	7	2
2NT	5	1
3♡	5	1
2♡	4	1
2♢	2	1

This is a familiar type of problem. Like the majority I voted for one spade, because neither two hearts nor three hearts nor three diamonds looks right. But next time I hold the hand I am going to try Armstrong's 2NT.

42

Bridge World
Director: Albert Morehead

Pairs, both vul. You, South, hold:

> ♠ K 9 4
> ♡ Q 10 8 6 2
> ◇ 8 7 4
> ♣ A J

South	West	North	East
—	—	—	1♡
No	1NT	No	2♣
No	No	dble	No
?			

You are pleased that partner has reopened, but what are you going to do now? Take a chance on beating two clubs or aim for a part-score your way? If so, in what denomination?

ERDOS: 2♠. This is close. A pass would be a terrific gamble, because dummy might well have four clubs and a singleton heart. If I could or would open a trump, I might pass, but from this specific holding a trump lead might be suicidal. Also, if they make it, partner will be reluctant to balance next time, so I play it safe and bid two spades.

This seems sensible enough, and there were others who took the same view.

HANNA: 2♠. In this sequence South should assume that North holds four spades; thus South should be happy to get to what is probably an excellent contract.

Director: A fine analysis, in one way. South could have made two spades.

OAKIE: 2♠. My partner shouldn't have any trouble reading this bid.

It's not likely that he would go to the three level in any event. A different view:

REMEY: Pass. Strictly a gamble, but declarer may have trouble ruffing his losing hearts, and I am willing to take a chance to get the 200 number.

This gave the Director an opening to express his own answer to the problem.

A gamble, undoubtedly; but since when aren't almost all bidding decisions gambles? Our point is that it's a good gamble, not a wild shot; and while we're on this subject, why is it that most experts will take all sorts of chances in offensive bidding but crawl into their shells where a penalty double is involved? We just don't get it.

Yes, I think that's a very interesting remark. Players are always ready to take a chance at game level but are wary of borderline doubles of a part-score contract. The vulnerability is always important. Here South may reflect that to take 100 won't be a good result against North–South pairs who have scored 110, but 200 on a part-score deal is 'jam'.

The problem, it was said, arose from the following deal:

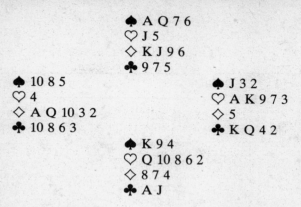

```
                    ♠ A Q 7 6
                    ♡ J 5
                    ◇ K J 9 6
                    ♣ 9 7 5
♠ 10 8 5                            ♠ J 3 2
♡ 4                                ♡ A K 9 7 3
◇ A Q 10 3 2                       ◇ 5
♣ 10 8 6 3                         ♣ K Q 4 2
                    ♠ K 9 4
                    ♡ Q 10 8 6 2
                    ◇ 8 7 4
                    ♣ A J
```

South led a low spade against two clubs doubled and the contract was one down. Note that the West hand contained both the features anticipated by Erdos – a singleton heart and four trumps.

This was the marking:

CALL	AWARD	PANEL
2♠	100	24
Pass	80	11
2♡	50	7
2◇	50	4
2NT	50	3

Morehead was contemptuous of two hearts, though this would have played quite well. Two diamonds is a poor answer, because this was likely to be West's long suit. Since South had only three cards in both spades and diamonds there was certainly a good case for aiming at 200 in two clubs doubled.

43

Bridge World
Director: Kit Woolsey

Pairs, E–W vul. You, South, hold:

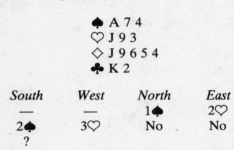

♠ A 7 4
♡ J 9 3
♢ J 9 6 5 4
♣ K 2

South	West	North	East
—	—	1♣	2♡
2♣	3♡	No	No
?			

Director: This is a very common type of matchpoint problem. The opponents have outbid you, and partner has passed the decision back to you. You have some extra values, but no clear course of action.

The passers believe that they have done justice to the hand.

COHN: Pass. Don't tell the same story twice.

WEISS: Pass. I've told my story. If partner were Roth, I'd double.

He means, because Roth favours sound opening bids and defends very keenly.

RUBENS: Pass. The shorter the tournament, and the larger the field, and the weaker my pair, the more likely I would be to double.

I do not agree that South has told his whole story. He is near maximum for his raise. True, game is out of the question, but that does not mean that South should meekly sell. North–South certainly can expect to make two spades, so either plus 100 or minus 140 at three hearts figures to be well below average. South must act if he intends to get his share of match-points on the board.

KOYTCHOU: 3♠. No comment.

RUBIN: 3♠. Playing five-card majors, three spades seems mandatory, since nobody knows who can make what.

Why should they make three hearts? We have at least half the deck, and the hands appear to be relatively balanced. If three hearts is not making, there is no question about the winning action. I strongly agree with the following panelists.

HEITNER: Double. This seems clear-cut at match-points. We have the balance of power; I have a good hand for defence, and partner's failure to compete suggests a balanced hand. Minus 140 rarely scores more than 25 per cent of the match-points, so I might as well go for the throat and double.

MCCALLUM (Karen): Double. Classic match-point double. If I'm right, it's a full-board swing. If I'm wrong I haven't cost much.

KOKISH: Double. Better to have the ace outside our own trump suit, but their vulnerability suggests enterprise, so let's live a little with an action double.

ROTH: Double. Match-point double! Looking for a one-trick set, but partner is allowed to take it out.

LEVIN: Double. Minus 140 or plus 100 will not be a good score, so I must gamble. Partner is not barred anyway. I'll only apologize if they make 930.

The Director may be right that in pairs a double is the best move. But this is his final comment:

These last panelists say or imply that North will pull the double with an appropriate hand. I strongly disagree. If North thought it was incorrect to defend three hearts, he would have bid three spades. It makes no sense for him to pass the decision to South (who might pass it out), and then pull to three spades when South announces that his hand is defensively oriented, with extra strength.

There is another way of looking at this type of competitive situation. Suppose that North has a 6–1–4–2 type, better in attack than defence: it may be good tactics for him to pass three hearts, intending to revert to spades if partner doubles three hearts. Then, if opponents go to four hearts, South will know how to assess his partner's hand.

This was the marking:

CALL	AWARD	PANEL
Double	100	18
3♠	60	7
Pass	50	7

For my part, I consider the double intelligent but risky, three spades understandable, pass weak.

Suppose the score were the other way round – your side vulnerable, they not. Double is not good now, because to take 100 instead of 50 might make very little difference.

44

Bridge Magazine
Director: Phillip Alder

IMPs, both vul. You, South, hold:

♠ 10 4
♡ A Q 8 7 6 3
◇ 7 2
♣ J 5 3

South	West	North	East
—	—	4♠	4NT
No	5◇	No	6◇
?			

It might have been a good move on South's part to bid five spades over East's 4NT. You would probably go to five spades over five clubs or five diamonds by the opposition, and it might be good tactics to force them to a decision a round earlier. However, no one made this point, so let's consider the problem that has arisen.

There are four possible calls: pass, double, six hearts, six spades.

Director: Do we save or not? If we do, should we indicate that we want a heart lead in case they get their wires crossed and move on to seven?

NORTH: 6♡. I am inclined to think that my expert opposition has got it right. If that is so, then it is correct to save. *En route*, it costs nothing to indicate a lead should they (unwisely) press on to seven.

WOLFF: 6♡. Unless South is a notorious overbidder, I opt to continue taking some insurance against seven diamonds by directing a heart lead.

Is it likely that they will bid seven missing the ace of hearts? The only time they might would be if East held ace of spades and a void in hearts. Is there, then, any tactical point in bidding six hearts?

CROWHURST: 6♠. Okay, I'll buy it. If East has taken an enormous yahoo and West is doomed to certain defeat, I may have to make one of my rare apologies to partner. On the surface, however, it looks as though East has taken the right view: both minor suits are breaking favourably and it is inconceivable that his hand contains two immediate major-suit losers. Three off in six spades should be cheap at the price.

Not everyone was willing to pay this cheap price.

REESE: Pass. You do not sacrifice, obviously, and partner is quite likely to lead a heart from a singleton or doubleton.

MORATH: Pass. When the opponents have been forced to guess, why assume that they have done the right thing? I could easily have two heart tricks.

A sage comment, indeed.
Some thought it necessary to double.

BENJAMIN: Double. If East has the likely three-suiter, North should be encouraged to lead his singleton heart.

ROWLANDS: Double. A guess, but my faith in their bidding does not extend to sacrificing, and since I do not want pard to lead a spade, double seems a justifiable risk.

I think that pard is likely to lead a heart whether you double or not. He can be sure that the opponents, unless playing a very deep game, will have spade control.

But now it turns out that East–West *were* playing a deep game.

HIRON: 6♡. It is difficult for me to be objective as I know the hand. In fact they were missing two aces – East knew it but

140

judged (correctly) that North–South would save. I don't for a moment expect them to bid seven, but stranger things have happened. Not often.

How honest can you get! He knows the slam had no chance but still he saves. Perhaps at the table he was East and wants to prove how clever his bid was.

This was the marking:

CALL	AWARD	PANEL
Pass	10	14
Dble	6	3
6♠	4	2
6♡	3	3

There might have been more discussion about the expected nature of the East hand. Does 4NT over four spades indicate a three-suiter or, initially, a two-suiter? There must be a chance, I would have thought, to find East with something such as:

♠ —   ♡ K J 10   ◇ A K x x x   ♣ A K Q x x

In any case, South's strong hearts surely represent a chance of defeating six diamonds. In general, I am hostile to slam sacrifices when my side has pre-empted and the opponents may have done the wrong thing.

Is there a case for doubling six diamonds to attract a heart lead? I doubt it, and if you are wrong you have presented them with an extra 170, which may mean 5 IMPs. Also, I am not sure that a double after this sort of sequence would be lead-directing.

45

Bridge International
Director: David Bird

Pairs, N–S vul. You, South, hold:

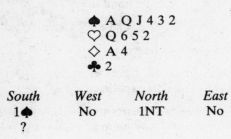

♠ A Q J 4 3 2
♡ Q 6 5 2
♢ A 4
♣ 2

South	West	North	East
1♠	No	1NT	No
?			

You may think this is a simple question, with an obvious answer. So do I. Nevertheless, the panel divided into two sections, plus a couple of oddities.

Director: Do we rebid the eminently respectable spade suit, keeping a close guard on our pairs plus score, but risking a missed game in hearts? Or do we rebid two hearts, possibly ending in an inferior part-score if partner passes? Two-thirds of the panel head for the spade suit.

MCNEIL: 2♠. Simon and Harrison-Gray are no doubt positively swirling in their graves, but bitter experience has told me that this is not a two-suiter.

Where did he get that idea? Simon sometimes made eccentric bids and Gray sometimes overbid, but neither would have dreamed of bidding anything but two spades here.

BENJAMIN: 2♠. Two hearts might strike oil, but it is ludicrous to request preference.

SHARPLES: 2♠. Even with some sort of heart fit the hand is probably best played in spades.

PARRY: 2♠. These hands usually play better in the long suit and two spades may be more comfortable than two hearts even facing four-card heart support.

Good on you, as I believe the Australians say. However, there were some doubtful supporters.

ROWLANDS: 2♠. Two hearts might turn out better but it looks against the odds. Alter the hand to

$$\spadesuit \text{ Q x x x x x} \quad \heartsuit \text{A Q J x} \quad \diamondsuit \text{A x} \quad \clubsuit \text{x}$$

and I would rebid two hearts.

Would you now? I would have thought it all the more important, with these plebeian spades, to play in the long suit.

COHN: 2♠. Change the 6 of hearts to the 10 and I will change my vote to two hearts. Any jump in spades deserves a zero.

You must speak louder. The next competitor did not hear you.

MOLLO: 3♠. Doing what comes naturally.

Also to Lavings [editor of the Australian magazine], but not to the rest of the panel. Let's hear the case for two hearts.

SOLOWAY: 2♡. Close choice, but partner might have hearts and a singleton spade and pass our spade bid.

Paul, I've just noticed that you bid exactly the same as Kantar on every single problem.

So we don't know whom to blame.

HIRON: 2♡. Yes, I am sure to be outvoted – all the wooden-tops will choose two spades and the nutters three spades. As I *know* that two hearts must be the right bid, I can afford 'one vote for two hearts (Hiron)' followed by a critical diatribe from the moderator.

From which one may judge that he knows it was silly.

KELSEY: 2♡. May strike the jackpot.

And may strike bottom.

KANTAR: 2♡. Clearer at IMPs.

He means that, playing in a team event, he would be more disposed to make the bid that might lead to a reasonable game contract. But minus 200, undignified at teams, is disastrous at pairs.

This was the marking:

CALL	AWARD	PANEL
2♠	10	14
2♡	5	7
3♠	2	2

It is odd, and presumably significant in some way, that the majority of the overseas panelists voted for two hearts. It seems to me that this will gain only if partner has a *marked* preference for hearts – such as a singleton spade and four or five hearts. That is possible, of course, but if partner just has *more* hearts than spades – say ♡ J x x and ♠ x x – two hearts will be a much inferior contract. And even if he has four hearts and one or two spades it is by no means certain that hearts will play better.

46

Australian Bridge
Director: Keith McNeil

Pairs, E–W vul. You, South, hold:

♠ K 10 6
♡ A 10 9 8
♢ Q 9 8 5 2
♣ 10

South	West	North	East
—	1♡	dble	No
?			

Director: Another hard decision to make, with a plethora of calls each having one or more defect.

Many of the calls he suggested had less than one merit, so let's see how the panel viewed this not unfamiliar problem.

ALDER: 2NT. To be honest, the best bid comes from the Roman Club system – two clubs exclusion, showing length in all suits except clubs.

Yes, that would help.

BOARDMAN: 3♢. Would like to bid 1NT (in my system 9–11 points in response to a double), but my singleton club is a problem.

The theory about notrump responses being strong was current in the 1930s, certainly. It just doesn't work when you are responding to a double of one heart (or one spade). What do you do with a 3–4–3–3 type, the only values in the suit that has been doubled?

CUMMINGS: 1NT. Pass is tempting, but trying to penalize at the level of one is a policy full of disillusionment. 1NT, though off-shape, is the best valuation available.

Another reactionary.

ROTH: 2♡. If partner bids two spades or three clubs, I plan on bidding three diamonds.

Ever onward.

MARSTON: 3◇. Seems dead obvious, although given the starchy view that most Australians have as to what constitutes a take-out double, perhaps I should be doing more. It is wrong not to use your most useful defensive bid often enough and your overcalling structure is burdened with the hands that should have been handled by a double.

There may be something in that, but the standards for take-out doubles are firm in most parts of the world.

MILES: 1♠. If partner passes we should be in a high-scoring partial. Game is unlikely unless partner can bid over one spade.

The Director didn't like this at all, observing:

As the non-jump suit bid denies 7–8 points, if partner does bid again you will have a lot to pick up.

Denies 7–8 points? I think that's much too wide a generalization.

LILLEY: Pass. Plus 200 is too much of a temptation to resist.

And minus 160 too much of a misery to contemplate. Also, plus 200 won't compensate for a missed game.

SHERMAN: 2◇. Even my paprika-charged blood chills at the thought of passing.

Well, you have seen examples of all seven choices now – and pretty ghastly some of them are. More intelligent:

146

SILVER: 2NT. 1NT is a gross underbid, two hearts is a gross overbid, and three diamonds practically rules out getting to the notrump game.

This was the marking:

CALL	AWARD	PANEL
3♦	100	12
2NT	90	7
1NT	80	9
Pass	70	1
2♡	60	2
1♠	10	1
2♦	10	1

The Director himself was very jolly about the majority choice of three diamonds. This expresses the values, I dare say, but has the disadvantage that it may not help you to get to the most likely game, 3NT. If partner has a fair hand with only a doubleton diamond he may decide to pass and you may miss an easy game in notrumps or spades.

My own vote was for 2NT, though I didn't express it as well as the Canadian (Joe Silver). And despite the Director's low opinion of the bid, I can see merit in Marshall Miles's one spade. If partner can find another bid you will have room in which to find the best contract.

PART VI
THE FIRST VOLLEY

Many of the magazine competitions also contain an occasional lead problem, which, of course, is related to the bidding. A few examples are included in this section.

47

Bridge World
Director: Alfred Sheinwold

IMPs, none vul. You, South, hold:

> ♠ 9 8 7 4
> ♡ Q J 4
> ◇ J 7
> ♣ A Q 10 6

South	West	North	East
—	—	—	1◇
No	1♠	No	1NT
No	2NT	No	No
No			

What do you lead?

The American style, at any rate at the time when this problem was devised, was to use strong notrumps at any score. Thus East is marked with a minimum opening and West with about 10 to 11 points.

Director: It will probably be difficult to beat 2NT since suits are apparently breaking fairly well for declarer. It seems to me that the best chance for the defence is to find a suit of their own – hearts or clubs. Since it's utter madness to tackle the clubs, South must obviously lead the queen of hearts.

So-called Roman leads, queen from K–Q, jack from Q–J, were not in vogue at this time.

The best comment on the lead was made by the sage of San José:

OAKIE: ♡Q. Let others tell why they wouldn't lead hearts.

Our man in San Berdoo (Bernadino) accepts the challenge.

MILES: ♠9. The *disadvantage* in leading a spade is that it may pick up partner's queen or jack. The alternative, the queen of hearts, is also dangerous. The deciding factor is that if I lead the queen of hearts, even if it doesn't cost a trick in the suit, partner may misjudge my heart length and try to set up the suit instead of switching to clubs.

And our tiger in New York shows how to solve this problem by confusing partner.

STERN: ♡J! I must attack hearts immediately to allow for partner's heart king and pointed winner (spades or diamonds). But the queen-lead is dangerous not so much because it *exposes* my jack to declarer as because it *reveals* the jack to partner. It is imperative that partner switch to clubs.

This prompted Alfy to recall his (distant) classical education:

'*The Athenians do not mind a man being clever,*' Plato once wrote, '*so long as he does not impart his cleverness to others.*'

This was the marking:

LEAD	AWARD	PANEL
♡Q	100	23
♠9	60	9
♡J	40	1
♣6	20	1

I'm sorry we were not told the reasoning of the panelist who proposed the 6 of clubs. Oh well, fourth best from your longest and strongest suit . . .

Sheinwold made no comment about the lead of the 9 of spades. My experience with this type of lead, from four small through dummy's suit, is that it seldom achieves anything and often costs a trick. Compare these two situations:

(1)   K 10 x
     A Q x x   J x
             9 8 7 x

Here the 9 will run to the jack and East may bring down North's king on a later round, making three tricks in the suit.

(2)   K 10 x
     J x   A Q x x
             9 8 7 x

Now the lead of the 9 into declarer's suit gives nothing away and stands to establish two tricks for the defence.

Thus I don't like the spade lead on the present deal, but what of Stern's jack of hearts? I am surprised that more panelists did not suggest this. For one thing, nothing is more annoying than to make a short-suit lead and receive encouragement from a partner who holds A x x or K x x. The defenders sometimes plug away at a suit of this kind, losing both tricks and tempo. So, when you do *not* want to imply that your suit is a good one, there is much to be said for a deceptive choice of card. If you decide to lead from K Q x against 3NT, the queen is less likely than the king to lead to an embarrassing sequel. Of course, if you normally play Roman leads (jack from Q–J, etc.), you will lead the top card in these situations.

48

Bridge World
Director: Robert Wolff

Pairs, none vul. You, South, hold:

♠ J 10 2
♡ 8 6 2
◇ K 10 9
♣ Q 9 3 2

South	West	North	East
—	1◇	No	1♠
No	2♣	No	3NT
No	No	No	

What do you lead?

It is a very common situation – the sort that causes many
players to go up and down their hands like a harpist, thus making
it clear that whatever they eventually lead is far from powerful.

Director: Let us begin with some unpopular choices.

ROGOFF: ♣2. Partner did not overcall, so he cannot hold more
than four decent hearts or five poor ones. East did not
investigate with fourth-suit forcing, so he has at least a
double stopper in hearts, quite possibly a triple stopper as
the cards lie. A decent club holding in partner's hand seems
to offer the most potential.

*He doesn't even mention the spade-jack lead. If you do lead
spades, is the jack the right card? No, says*

KOKISH: ♠2. There's a fair chance that West is 1–3–5–4 or
1–4–4–4, or the like. The spade *two* may catch dummy with

a singleton *honour*, letting us build an internal spade trick or two, to hold down overtricks; it just might be vital not to blow our pips. This combines safety with some real home-run potential.

The 2 might also (a) mislead partner, (b) lead to a block in the run of the suit. Most spade leaders went for the natural card.

JAQUES: ♠J. East's hearts are good, and his spades may be very feeble.

MILES: ♠J. I need only find partner with Q 9 x x for spades to be a good lead. In hearts, he would need a much stronger holding.

HARDY: ♠J. Partner, who did not overcall, cannot have good hearts, but he can have good enough spades to make this lead golden.

ROTH: ♠J. Might hit a lucky strike.

Yes, you might. More likely, you'll blow critical overtricks.

BLACKWOOD: ♡8. A heart lead has the best chance of giving nothing away; anything else is dangerous. The 8 asks partner to try a different suit when he gets the lead.

CARAVELL: ♡8. We are unlikely to beat them – the object is to give away nothing on the opening lead. I suppose the spade jack could work out, but when I make such leads the dummy has a singleton or doubleton queen and declarer has A 9 8 7 x. The totally passive lead seems best.

RUBIN: ♡6. Partner probably owns enough cards to overcall had he a five-card major, so the heart lead probably won't strike oil. The other reasonable leads are the spade jack and club 2, but neither is appetizing. So, retreat to the heart 6.

Those are my sentiments exactly. It's not that I love the heart lead more, it's just that I like the alternatives less.

This was the marking:

LEAD	AWARD	PANEL
♠J	100	13
♡8	90	9
♡6	90	3
♠2	60	1
♡2	50	1
♣2	40	3
♢10	20	0

Almost half, including the distinguished Director, opt for a heart! That's the effect, I suppose, of playing in a very match-point-conscious atmosphere, where the objective, when you don't expect to beat the contract, is not to give away a trick with the lead. I tried it on Martin Hoffman, an outstanding pairs player, and he too winced at the suggestion of so negative an attack.

The spade lead might turn out well, but declarer probably has five spades and you are gambling that the dummy will have a singleton.

The best *attacking* lead is the *queen* of clubs – not the 2. The queen may pin a singleton jack or 10 in the declarer's hand. Also, it is deceptive. Sorry if you think it's silly!

49

British Bridge World
Director: Alan Truscott

IMPs, both vul. You, South, hold:

> ♠ J
> ♡ 4 3
> ◇ K 10 9 8 5
> ♣ J 9 6 5 3

South	West	North	East
—	—	1♡	2♡
No	3NT	No	6♣
No	No	dble	No
No	No		

What do you lead?

This is not the greatest – or, at any rate, the most difficult – problem of all time, but wait for the finish!

Director: This was a hand from the Schwab Cup in 1933 – long before Mr Lightner had thought of his famous double. There are two sound reasons for playing the doubler for a club void rather than a diamond void.

SWINNERTON-DYER: ♣3. Partner appears to have a minor-suit void and one other trick, for he can hardly be counting on any contribution from me. The question is, which void? There are two pointers, each of which should lead to the right answer. In the first place, if partner has a diamond void I shall almost certainly make a trick by force in the suit, and so need not bother about partner's ruff. In the second place, East must have a big semi two-suiter, and his second suit (where the ruff is coming) is likely to be pretty solid. So it can hardly be diamonds, in view of my holding in the suit.

Truscott, incidentally, was well off the mark when he said that the Lightner double was not in vogue at the time of the Schwab Cup in 1933. The *Bridge Encyclopaedia* (of which he was Executive Editor) gives the date as 1929.

This was the marking:

LEAD	AWARD	PANEL
♣	10	10
♢	3	1
♡	2	1

No other comments were quoted – or, indeed, were needed, but this was the final paragraph:

Filarski recalls having a similar problem when he played with F. Goudsmit in the European Championship at Copenhagen (1948). He gave his lead protracted thought, which would reduce most Lightner doublers to nail-biting. But Goudsmit remained cool, real cool – he held the A K of trumps!

50

Bridge World
Director: Jeff Rubens

Pairs, N–S vul. You, South, hold:

♠ A K 10 6 3
♡ 8 7
◇ Q 7 5
♣ 9 3 2

South	West	North	East
—	—	No	1♡
1♠	2♣	No	2NT
No	No	dble	No
No	No		

What do you lead?

Director: It is useful to have rules about lead-directing doubles. However, rules should hold sway only when logic is unavailable. If possible, common sense should determine the correct path. This is common sense here:

WOOLSEY: ♣9. For North, a passed hand, to have a double of 2NT on this auction, he *must* have both clubs and hearts locked up, so the club lead looks best.

STERN: ♣2. The only sure thing about partner's hand is that he has clubs bottled up; no reason to assume he expected me to make an aggressive lead.

Summarizing for common sense:

FREIER: ♣2. On this bidding I can't believe partner wants a

spade lead. A good club stack can be his only reason for a double. He probably holds good hearts also.

Yes, probably. But maybe partner is hoping South has a heart honour, or at least some sort of a hand (instead of the foot South actually has for his overcall).

Foot? Meaning rubbish? It's not in my thesaurus.

KATZ: ♣9. The problem is which club to lead. The deuce's only advantage is to give count, but partner will quickly get the club count the second time you lead through dummy – the declarer is a big favourite to show out.

But not everyone sees the issue as which club. Other suits made their appearance.

KANTAR: ♡8. I made a big bid on (a previous problem) and I'm making a big lead on this one.

EISENBERG: ♡8. Probably a club is all right.

Isn't that backwards? Shouldn't it be, 'Probably a heart is all right, but a club is guaranteed all right'.

This is a mild reply to a very improbable answer. North has passed originally and hearts have been bid on his left. Even if he has a holding such as Q J 10 9 x, how can he double 2NT and how can he expect his partner to lead a heart rather than a club? But one answer was so quaint that one must doubt whether he read the question correctly.

KOKISH: ◇7. Going for the big number. Partner rates to hold three goodish clubs, a heart lock, diamond length and spade shortage.

And the Crown jewels.
    I wonder, too, how a spade can be right. Nevertheless:

EWEN: ♠3. I play that a double of 3NT (*sic*) requires the lead of a suit bid by our side.

NASON: ♠6. You can never go wrong doing what partner tells you to do, on this type of auction.

Only if you got the right message.

This was the marking:

LEAD	AWARD	PANEL
♣9	100	13
♣2	90	9
♠6	50	8
♠K	40	3
♠3	40	1
♡8	30	2
♢7	20	1

There was a point in favour of ♣9, as against ♣2, that no one brought out. Suppose the club position were something like this:

```
                 A Q 10 6
   K J 8 5 4                    7
                 9 3 2
```

The 9 lead (if South can come in twice with his spade honours) picks up all four tricks.

Two other replies were a trifle mysterious:

SWANSON: ♠6. I am not in the habit of psyching vulnerable overcalls.

Jeff Rubens read this as a criticism of the one spade overcall. But perhaps the panelist meant: 'I bid spades, I have spades, and partner has asked me to lead a spade.'

And Ira Rubin seemed to think that a partner who had passed originally could not possibly have a sound double of 2NT:

RUBIN: Partner must be loony.

Aren't they all?